Legacy of Loneliness

Blood and Moonlight

Book 2

By Olyn Moon

STHENOTYPE

Cover art by Laura Farley
Editing by Michael Allen

First Edition 2025

ISBN 979-8-9923513-3-0

Published by SthenoType
Medford, NJ 08055
www.SthenoType.com

To everyone who enjoyed Legacy of Embers enough that they let me go further with these characters.

Chapter One

What's the first thing you'd do if you had the love of
your life in bed beside you while your other love spooned
you after a long week? Yea, I don't know either. After finding
out I wasn't human, I thought things would get easier. Less
complicated, at the very least. It turns out being married to
an Alpha to a werewolf pack and the Matriarch of a vampire
clan, life isn't all sunshine and daisies. It's a lot more like
navigating a minefield of supernatural politics and ancient
prejudices. My name is Rai. It's pronounced Ray; unless you're
Ash, then it's Rye, and I am a Phoenix. A creature of fire and
rebirth. Apparently, the child of two sun deities, according
to a now-dead original vampire Yujin. He had revealed what
I was in a letter after his untimely death to an old enemy.
I couldn't just ask them myself since I had been left on a
church step as a baby.

My husband, Ash, had undergone a ritual that had made
him the Alpha of his pack. The problem with that was that
his pack was not the closest, so he was gone every month
for days at a time during the full moon. He had just left that
morning, and his absence already left an ache in my heart.
The same ritual granted my wife, Tessa, the title of Matriarch
of her clan, which now roamed the mansion I had inherited.
Well, more forced, much to the dismay of Isiak, Tessa's uncle,
to have so that other vampires wouldn't be allowed in after
everything that happened last year.

And through all that, I had finals to study for. The
pressure mounted as the weight of exams poured over me. It

was hard to concentrate while my skin yearned for the woman lying deathly still on the bed behind me. I can't remember the last time I had been with either Ash or Tessa. Time had seemed to lose its meaning in the chaos that consumed our lives. I couldn't fully understand what they were going through. One moment, they were nobodies in a world I never knew existed, never once believing they would be more than what they were, and then authority was thrust upon them to unite a clan of werewolves and vampires. It was a completely impossible task. Which is why it had not worked out well at all. The animosity between the two groups was so palpable it felt alive. Some wolves had tried staying in the mansion, but the fighting amongst them and the vampire spiraled out of control. Ash and Tessa decided it would be better for the pack to go back home. It was a desperate decision—one I thought was wrong but had no say in.

Now, before I get any further, when I say married, it wasn't in the way you might think. The normal world, and conventional standards, wouldn't see it that way. Yujin had performed a bonding ritual that, in the eyes of the werewolves and vampires, was easiest explained as marriage. The ritual, steeped in ancient magic, had forged an unbreakable bond between Ash and Tessa's minds that let them see the others' memories and feelings. Being what I am, magic didn't work on me, but since I was part of the ceremony, the vampires and werewolves viewed me as part of that bond. A representative for the scions. It was a strange position to be in since I had no other demigods or gods to bring to this merger of supernatural beings. But despite that magic not working on me, it still brought an undeniable smile to my face as I thought of them both as mine and me as theirs.

But I digress. While the first month of living together had been full of promise and potential, the rest of the year had been much harsher, as reality set in. Isiak and his wife Corri had not been subtle with their outright hate that the youngest of the clan had jumped magnitudes ahead of them in power to become head of the clan. Their hostility didn't help the werewolf and vampire dispute the bond had meant to curb. I had no proof, but I was pretty sure they were the cause of all the ire. They threatened the unity that the bond had meant to create. The vampires that had made this their new home were less antagonistic towards their new Matriarch, but Isiak was still the oldest among them, and easily able to influence them with just his actions.

I closed my books and lay my head on the table. I needed some air, but the large house was far too quiet this early in the day. The stillness of the big house could be oppressive at times. With only the creaking of the old wood to keep me company, it was not the best place to be lost in thought. Even the maids slept in until noon. They, like most everyone else in this strange household, kept unusual hours. After a moment, I pushed away from the desk and made my way through the maze of halls to the side yard. I still never understood why vampires loved mazes. Caves and houses, no matter where I had been that were created by vampires, always seemed to be a maze of twisting halls. I still didn't know how to navigate the house, even after a year.

The house we lived in was almost in the center of town, but you wouldn't know it by the looks of it. You could walk to any of the major places, the college, the theater, the mall, and the grocery store quite easily. Whoever had built the place, I wasn't sure if it had been Isiak or not, wanted that feeling of isolation without being isolated. Filling an entire block, the house was enormous. The actual yard itself was relatively small, which I bet the gardeners enjoyed. An Olympic-sized swimming pool occupied the largest part of the yard. Around the property were large Grand Fir trees. They were dense enough to block sight and went back about thirty feet. The driveway even added to the sense of living in the wilderness. It took a few minutes to drive down the path to get to the house, and along the way, Monterey Cypress trees had created a tunnel-like effect down the entire drive. It felt like a scene from some fantasy or horror movie. You didn't know if you were stepping into a world of magic or going to die by some faceless slasher.

The sun was already beating down as I stepped outside at 9 A.M. I made my way to the pool to soak up some sun as I lay down on a large lounge chair. The distant sound of chirping birds and tree leaves that rustled in the dry wind created a serene backdrop for relaxation. I must have dozed off as I listened to the sounds. My body jerked awake from the feeling of falling. I fell off the lounge chair and landed on the hard concrete below. Dazed and disoriented, I couldn't get my thoughts straight, and it took me a minute to remember where I was. As I gathered my thoughts, a wave of unease washed over me. A shiver ran through me as the feeling that someone had been watching me crept over me. I looked up at the house, but the curtains were still drawn tightly shut. Still, that eerie feeling stayed. A loud cawing from the trees turned my attention that way. A solitary raven perched on a limb. As it took flight and disappeared into the distance, so did the uneasy presence that had lingered around me.

"I need a break," I groaned and stood up.

I groggily reached for my phone and saw the little light

flashing. It was a missed call from Ash. I was more shocked at what time it was. It was already after 3 P.M. and I hadn't expected to sleep for six hours. I shook away the sleepiness I still felt and called Ash back.

"Hey," he answered.

"How's everything going?" I asked.

"Oh, you know. Same old things. Got a couple of new pups tonight that I'll be staying with. My twin cousins. Remember them?" Ash asked.

"Not Jane and John? They were already wild enough," I laughed.

"The same ones. They're getting worse as the day goes on and the moon calls to them," groaned Ash. "But anyway, I wanted to just make sure you and Tessa are doing well."

"She's still asleep. I was, too, until just now. So, you think you're going to be staying away longer since they're new?" I asked.

"I don't know yet. The other older wolves have more experience. I just need to make them know I am the Alpha, so I gotta be here for their change. I imagine they're going to want to be leaders before long."

"Well, I hope you get back soon. I can't wait to touch your body," I purred into the phone.

"Stooop, my mom is two feet away," muttered Ash.

"That's what makes it so fun," I laughed loudly.

"Take care of yourself. We'll have plenty of fun when I get back."

As I listened to his voice, I could almost picture the

smile on his nice lips. His tan, muscled body was next to come to my mind. The twinkle in his ocean blue eyes always made me weak when he smiled. Alongside that dimple he got. The way he ran his hand through his short red hair when he was nervous. I sighed as he hung up and made my way back inside the house. It was still a few hours until the sun went down, and my stomach rumbled as it reminded me I hadn't even had lunch. Normally, I would cook myself something, but for once, I didn't feel like cooking. Instead, I decided I wanted to visit a place that I hadn't been to in weeks. Soon, I was sitting in a familiar red leather booth in a red and black checkered 50s-themed diner. The lunch rush was over, so it was mostly empty. Only one other person was there, and he looked familiar to me. As I waited for my burger and fries, my eyes kept drifting to the man as I racked my brain trying to figure out where I had seen him before. His hair was such an intense shade of blue that it almost appeared black. He had buzzed part of his hair on the left side and back; the rest fell messily over his right eye.

"Here ya go, darlin'," said an older woman as she handed me my food and a chocolate shake.

"Thank you," I smiled.

She smiled back and walked to the other person. As I was eating, voices rose.

"Try it again, please," pleaded the man.

"I've tried it three times already. Do you have anything else?" asked the waitress, clearly losing patience.

"No," the man replied as his shoulders slumped.

I walked over and handed the waitress my card.

"Here I got it," I offered. "Pay for mine while you have

it."

She glanced at me, then took it and walked away. The man met my gaze with shame before running off.

"No thanks are needed," I mumbled to myself and went back to my table.

The sun was slowly sinking below the horizon when I finally made it back home, and I felt much better. Surprisingly, despite my parents being gods of dawn, I felt much more reinvigorated at night. Then again, I did have a beautiful lover like Tessa to come home to. As I opened the door, she stood there with a smile across her pale red lips. She had pulled her long black hair, which normally covered her face, back into a messy bun, displaying her golden lip ring. Her green eyes danced with excitement. I smiled brightly and swept her up into a warm, loving embrace and lost myself in a long, passionate kiss. Having her in my arms filled me with a warmth and happiness I wish everyone could feel.

"Mmm, I can smell the burger on you still. Did you bring me one?" she smiled as she pulled away.

"Sorry, I'll make you one for dinner. Forgive me?" I asked sheepishly.

"Hmm, we will have to see how good it tastes," she smirked.

"Oh no, I shall start prepping right away so I can make it to your standards, milady," I joked.

"Don't you dare," she said and pulled me into another kiss.

I scooped her up into my arms, and she instinctively wrapped her legs around my waist. I pressed her against the wall as my lips found their way down her neck as I left a trail of kisses on her skin. She let out a soft moan and tilted her head back in pleasure. My hand found its way under her shirt and to her bra.

"Ahem," came a loud voice from our left.

I stopped and looked at Isiak.

"If you would be so kind as to take this debauchery somewhere not in the middle of our front door," he scoffed.

"Oh no, I'm being accused of debauchery by a vampire," I gasped. "Whatever will we do?"

I slid Tessa down the wall and backed away as she pouted.

"Why are you here?" asked Tessa.

"I do live here, child," said Isiak as he walked by us.

She pushed herself off the wall and sighed, "I should go get nourishment while you get ready for dinner tonight."

With one more quick kiss, she was gone. She still made sure I wasn't around to see her eating, but I knew she had finally found someone new to be her primary source. Keira Bennett was a nice person who had somehow discovered that vampires existed and came looking to be used as a feeding source. She rarely talked about where she came from, but I got the feeling that being a maid in a large mansion, and sometimes used for her blood, was much preferable to wherever she had come from. Her blonde pixie hair had grown out long enough to be put into a bun since she had joined us.

I went to the walk-in cooler and found some beef that I had ground earlier, then put it into a bowl. Once that was ready, I began a simple seasoning. Paprika, onion powder, garlic powder, freshly cracked pepper, salt, and just a tiny pinch of cayenne. I poured half of it into the bowl with the ground beef and gently mixed it all together to not overwork the meat. After thoroughly washing my hands, I peeled potatoes to turn them into steak fries. I saved the rest of the seasoning to use on the fries after frying them. Next, I sliced a tomato and an onion, shredded some fresh lettuce, and put a group of crinkled, crunchy pickles on a plate. Then I put a skillet over the stove's flames to let it heat as I formed the beef into patties. After forming the patties, I put a large pot of oil on another burner to bring it to a boil for the fries while the skillet warmed. I placed the patties into the skillet with a spatula, then reached for the buns and placed them onto a grill to toast.

When the bread was finished, I took them off and put two on each plate before I flipped the burgers. Carefully, I dropped a basket of fries into the pot of oil. While they fried, I assembled the buns. For mine, I spread mayo on the bottom and the top with mustard. Then I layered lettuce over the mayo, and pickles over the mustard, topped with two tomato slices. For both of Tessa's, I put ketchup on the bottom with two slices of tomatoes on the top bun. By the time I finished with the bread, the fries were golden. I pulled them out and let the oil drip. I put a slice of cheese on each burger and turned off the stove. As the cheese melted, I put fries on the bottom of Tessa's burger. I piled the rest of the fries onto my plate. Finally, I placed the burgers onto the buns and set the tops on.

I had just gotten done plating the food when Tessa returned. Her emerald eyes were glowing, and a smile tugged at her ruby lips.

"Someone woke up on the good side of the bed tonight," I said with a smile.

"I know I've been distant lately. Things have been hard, but I've decided all that can wait for tomorrow. I've missed you," she beamed at me.

"I can put off studying for a night. I already spent most of the day sleeping myself," I chuckled.

"Oh, are you saying I can't get you into my bed?" she purred from behind me as she wrapped her arms around me.

"Mmm, I don't know. I might be bribed," I grinned.

"Oh? What would it take?" she asked and ran her hands under my shirt.

As she ran her hands up my stomach, I shivered, and not just from the cold of her fingertips.

"You're just trying to distract me so that you don't have to forgive me for not bringing a burger," I squirmed and laughed.

"Caught red-handed," she said and kissed my neck. "Is it ready?"

"You made it just in time. Everything is perfect. I just need to get ketchup for my fries. Go sit down, and I will bring everything out."

She smiled at me and glided out of the kitchen without a sound. I smiled to myself and gathered everything onto a tray.

Chapter Two

Despite my desperate desire, the weekend went by too quickly. This year, I had been forced to take morning classes, which made Mondays the worst days ever. I spent Sunday nights with Tessa and Ash, when I got the chance to, that I couldn't bear going to sleep early enough to get any rest. The slam of a door jolted me awake that Monday morning, slightly before dawn, and chased away a dream that I forgot as soon as I realized I was awake. I sat up bleary-eyed and looked around for the sound that had caused me to wake up before my alarm.

"Sorry," Tessa said with her hand to her mouth.

"It's fine," I yawned. "What happened?"

I tapped next to me, and she crawled into bed beside me.

"I have to do something about my uncle, and I just don't know what to do. If I kill him, people will fear me while trying to overthrow me in secret. If I let him continue plotting against me in the open and do nothing, then it will make others brave enough to listen to him," she sighed, and buried her face in my chest.

I rubbed her back and said, "Can you, like, bury him alive for a century?"

"I don't know if it will work," she sighed. "No matter what I do, something bad is going to happen."

"What about controlling them like you did when you

11

left with them to find Cazimir?"

"Cause it's not real control. We were just in sync after our family members died."

"Oh," I murmured and hugged her tightly.

She lifted her head and kissed me softly. "I am sorry for waking you."

"It's fine, I swear."

Before long, she was in the dead-like state she slept in. I wriggled out from under, and as I checked my phone, I realized I had plenty of time for a shower and breakfast before heading to class. The hot water cascaded over my body as my thoughts wandered to Ash and what I wanted to do to his body. The shower lasted a little longer than I had intended. That made me settle on cereal for breakfast so that I could get to the campus early and get some extra studying done before the long day ahead. Sleepily, I yawned and made my way to the library. I walked across campus in a daze, warm morning light on my skin, when someone grabbed my hand. It took a moment for my brain to register the shorter woman in front of me, her skin a deep olive. She gazed up at me, her large gray eyes wide. She had shaved her dark blue hair on the left side, and it messily covered the right.

"What are you doing?" I exclaimed, startled.

"I just wanted to thank you. It took me a bit to realize it was you, and then you were ignoring me as I waved," she explained.

"Thank me for what? Can I have my hand back?" I asked, tugging slightly.

She released my hand, and I backed away. I looked

around, half-expecting to be ambushed.

"You paid my bill at the diner," she breathed.

"Um, I don't think that was me. Who are you?"

"My name's Casey. This is my first year."

"I think I've seen you around before. But I am sure I've never paid for anything you ate."

She slapped her head.

"I'm so stupid. I looked different. It's… hard to explain. Nobody ever really believes me. And when they find out… they leave me," she said with a sadness in her eyes that I knew all too well.

"I'm headed to the library if you want to try to explain it to me. I'll try to understand, though I will warn you I've not gotten a lot of sleep. But anything to not study alone," I said, walking off.

She ran to catch up with me and was quiet as we walked.

"Believe me when I say, nothing you could tell me could be weirder than my life," I said finally.

She stood quietly for a few more moments, but when she spoke, her voice was a bit deeper.

"I'm not what people would call normal," Casey said.

I turned, and the man I had paid the bill for stood beside me.

"Wha… where… how?" I stammered, glancing around. "Twin sister?"

"No," he replied. "I'm still the same person."

"You've got to be lying. You're not even the same

13

height. And don't even get me started on how your jawline is sharper," I sighed.

"You're staring at my jawline now?" he asked with a raised brow.

"No... I... who are you, really?"

"Like I said. I'm Casey Nielsen. And... usually I don't switch when I'm with other people. Who are you?"

"I'm just Rai. Nothing special about me. What do you mean switch? Like two personalities?"

"If only that was the case. No. Ever since I was a kid, I could swap my gender whenever I was feeling like the other didn't suit me. I ended up being homeschooled and made to stay inside a lot. When I wasn't being called a freak by my mother's family," Casey said as he looked away.

"What about your father?" I asked.

"Didn't have one. My mother wouldn't talk about him. And since he left me without bothering to care, I don't even want to meet him," Casey growled.

"Sorry to bring it up. So, you can shapeshift? Can you control it?" I asked.

"It's not as simple as that. I can't do it at will. It just... happens."

"That's not the weirdest thing I've heard," I mumbled.

"That's not usually the reaction I get," he said skeptically. "Most people freak out when I show up looking like a twin to someone they just met."

"I can't say what it's like to not have friends, but I know someone who is lonely when I see them. I can't imagine a life

14

like yours, but I'm not gonna run away from you. Not after what I've been through myself. I'm happy to be your friend."

I stuck out a hand, and he stared down at it in disbelief.

"This isn't a trick," I said.

He shook my hand, and I smiled.

"I will pay you back, I promise. I'm just having trouble this year with tuition and it's hard finding a job when you get fired for not showing up, even when you did," he said.

"Hmm, and your mother can't do that whole switching thing?" I asked.

"Not that she's ever mentioned to me. She hasn't talked to me since I told her I was going to college. She fully expected me to stay locked up in our hometown."

"Well, me and you are good. Don't worry about paying me back, and I don't plan on leaving this town anytime soon, so if things get too rough with rooms, I have a large house."

"You're rich?" he asked.

"Not so much. It was basically willed to me after someone I knew died."

"Oh. I'm sorry," he said.

"It's fine. It's been a while," I waved him off.

I motioned for them to sit on a bench.

"Thought you were going to the library?" he asked.

"Well, I figured you could just use someone to hang out with. I'm… not the most experienced with things like talking, but I've got an hour to kill before my day actually starts."

He sat down as I did.

15

"So, what brought you to this college?" I asked as I racked my brain to say anything.

"Mostly to get away, and this place was the only place I got accepted to. There's something strange about this place. People avoid me a lot and not in the normal way," he muttered.

I looked around, and everyone was giving us a wide berth. The werewolves that I knew were gone because of the moon cycle. But even the normal students seemed to avoid us. That was new to me; most people here just seemed to act like I didn't exist.

"I'm sure it's nothing. These people around here aren't so bad. The surf team's coach is a nice guy, if you can get past his shaggy looks and permanent angry-looking face," I fumbled my words.

"That guy is the surfing coach? He's hulking and looks like he should be in a metal band."

"Don't tell him that. I made that mistake once, and he chewed me out on judging appearances," I laughed.

"Duly noted," he said with a chuckle.

"Do you often go to that diner? I don't think I've ever seen you there before."

"It was my first time, to be honest."

"It's the best place around. If you want milkshakes, oh man, they make the best bar none," I said.

"I'll try to remember that," he laughed.

We spent the rest of the time in surprisingly comfortable silence—at least until it was time for me to go. The rest of the day seemed to stretch on endlessly as my eyelids grew heavier. Through the small breaks between classes, I had to resist the urge to take a nap. I almost gave in to that feeling during lunch, but I knew that if I did, I would have slept through any alarm. As I went from class to class, I didn't cross paths with Casey again. While I was on my way home, my phone rang as Ash called me.

"Hello, handsome," I said as I answered the phone.

"Hey there, hottie," teased Ash. "How was the first day of finals?"

"Don't bring that up," I groaned. "I'm so exhausted."

"Didn't you get enough sleep?"

"Not even close. Isiak is getting out of hand," I sighed.

"She needs to do something about him if she wants him to stop undermining her," growled Ash.

"I guess… if she's going to keep others in line," I muttered. "How are the twins?"

"They were feisty, but I think they'll be fine. I spent all night chasing them down, so I'm just waking up," he explained. "But don't change the subject. If I don't help her, then they won't respect me as partly their leader. Since the whole bonded by magic thing."

"Maybe," I said half-heartedly. "I'm gonna go home and take a nap, I'll call you tonight."

"Just be safe in there. They might try to use you somehow and force her to make a choice. I'll be home when I can."

"I will. I don't think Isiak wants to die. He just wants to lead."

"If I didn't think he'd abuse that power, I would try to convince her to let him have it."

"Just get home soon, I miss your face."

Chapter Three

The moon had risen high into the clear sky when I finally stirred from my nap. The sound of raised angry voices had woken me. I followed the echoes as they drew me down the halls and to the empty room that had once belonged to Yujin.

"I am not breaking an alliance with the werewolves," growled Tessa as I listened from behind the door.

"They are foul creatures who want to do nothing but kill us. They are our antithesis, and being around them is nothing but trouble. The other vampires want to leave because of the one who is always here as it is," Isiak said coolly.

"Ash has done nothing to them. They will learn to accept him," I heard the boiling anger in Tessa's voice.

"We are not meant to be near them. This alliance was meant to be a temporary thing. Yujin even said it himself. It was to save us from Cazimir."

"Grandfather didn't always know what was best. I'm also not him."

"He knew better than you, child," Isiak said with a heavy sigh, "And so do I. I don't know how much longer I can keep our family under control. Some have already left to find out darker kin."

"Did you take care of them? We can't allow someone who can come into the house to be turned."

19

"Of course."

I slowly shuffled back from the closed door and intended to go back to my room. My mind spun in confusion. Tessa had been lying to me the whole time. Isiak was not the main issue, like I thought he was. It was everyone else who had caused all the small problems that kept adding up. My mind raced as it tried to reconcile this fact. Tessa and Isiak were always fighting when I saw them. Now that I thought about it, I had noticed that the house seemed a bit emptier. I hadn't thought anything about it, honestly. Suddenly, I found myself outside instead of in my room, and I kept walking. Only one thing was clear to me: I needed to be away from everyone inside right now. So, of course, I went to the one place that I knew would be open, Stardust. It was the diner that I'd come to love. The neon sign beckoned me and told me that it would be my sanctuary from the chaos that swirled inside me while my mind tried to wrap around what I heard. I eagerly pushed open the door with hopes to try to put the drama at home out of my mind.

"What can I get ya?" asked Mary, the waitress.

"I'm still deciding," I lied.

I wasn't there for the food or milkshakes, I just couldn't be home. Eventually, I'd have to order something, but the churning in my gut made it hard to even attempt to think of anything on the menu. I kept the menu up, pretending to read while I just stared down at the table, hiding my face.

"It's kinda late, isn't it?" came a female voice from across the booth.

I lowered the menu and was surprised to see Casey sitting across from me. Her chin was in the palm of her hands, and her elbows were on the table.

"I took an extra-long nap," I mumbled. "I'm not tired."

"Yea, I can't sleep either. Though I didn't expect to see you here when I came back," she said. "Don't worry, I have money this time."

"That's good," I replied as I put the menu back up.

"Did I do something?" she asked with a tremble in her voice.

"No, I'm just… It's been a bad night."

I heard her get up to leave, and I lowered the menu and grabbed her arm.

"You can stay," I whispered. "I'm sorry. You didn't do anything. Maybe we can get something to eat."

She smiled, and I couldn't help but return a faint smile. I waved the waitress over.

"You ready darlin'?" she asked.

"I am. Can I have a strawberry shake, and my friend will have…" I glanced over at Casey.

"Can I have cheese fries?" she asked.

"Coming right up," Mary smiled.

She took the menu and walked away.

"So, can I help with your issue?" Casey asked, her tone gentle but curious.

"Not really. What brings you here this late?"

"My roommate was snoring loud enough to wake the dead," she answered. "In fact, I'm pretty sure her small animal skull collection shook."

When the fries and milkshake arrived, we sat quietly for a bit, enjoying the treats in front of us.

"Oh right," she said suddenly, standing up. "I need to show you my cat. Socks."

She slid next to me in the booth and took her phone out. I leaned closer. Her background screen showed a graying black cat with white paws. She opened a folder filled with pictures. Socks as a kitten to adult, curled in blankets, climbing shelves, mid-yawn.

"I've had her since… god, I was like five," she said as she scrolled.

One photo was a kid with bright blue hair cuddling a tiny black kitten with white paws. A younger Casey and Socks.

"What an original name," I laughed.

"Hey now! Like I said, I was five," she pouted.

I nudged her slightly with my shoulder and smiled. She looked down and ate a fry.

"You can have some if you want," she said as she slid the plate between us.

"Thanks," I grabbed one and bit into it.

My phone buzzed in my pocket, but I ignored it as Casey kept scrolling through more cat photos. The time rolled by as I watched the cat grow along with her.

"That kitten must have gotten you through a lot of tough times," I said.

"For the longest time, she was my only friend," she mumbled. "I hope my mother is taking care of her."

"Have you thought about going to see her and your

mother for the summer?" I asked.

"I did, but she wouldn't let me leave if I did that."

"Is she that bad?"

"She's not bad. She cared for me, despite my condition, after all. Just overprotective. She doesn't think that I will make it out here in the real world. Something inside me is calling me here. This school was just the first step. I don't know what it is, but since I've been here, that feeling has just gotten stronger."

"This is the town to find a calling, that's for sure," I muttered as I remembered last year.

I still had nightmares about zombie attacks. I still wasn't sure how Cazimir had sent them after me, but I hadn't been attacked since he had died.

"Do you have experience with something like that?"

"Just with weird things from this town in general," I shrugged. "I can't truly say that I've had that same call, but this town has changed my life forever."

She gave me a curious tilt of her head.

"It's too much to explain, and maybe not in this diner," I breathed.

"Oh," she said and looked around the empty diner.

The bell on the door jingled as it opened and drew my attention. I sighed heavily as Isiak walked in.

"I gotta go," I said as I stood up.

Casey looked at me, then at Isiak, and I saw the shudder run down his body as he looked into Isiak's eyes.

"There you are," came the boyish, singsong voice.

I walked by him without saying a word. I didn't hear him, but I knew he would follow.

"Who is the new friend? Should I keep it a secret?" Isiak asked as he appeared in step beside me.

"Why would you need to keep it a secret?" I asked as I looked over at him.

"Well, Tessa was worried when you didn't answer your phone, and you disappeared without a word. She thought someone had kidnapped you. But there you were, with another person."

"I didn't know she was going to be there," I said with a shrug. "I just wanted some air, then got hungry."

"She?" he asked.

"He, I meant," I stuttered and looked away.

"Interesting," he muttered.

He didn't say anything else until we got back home.

"I found him!" Isiak yelled as he opened the door.

When I stepped into the foyer, I was wrapped up in a huge hug from Tessa.

"You're safe!" she cried, the relief flooding her voice.

Then she released me, only to slap my arm with the front and back of her hand.

"Where were you? Why did you leave? It's almost 2 am! Then you never answered your phone. I thought someone had gotten to you," she said, her voice breaking with tears.

"I'm sorry," I said softly and put my arms loosely around her waist.

She wrapped her arms around me again. Her body

trembled as she cried against my chest. After a moment, I took her hand and led her to our room. As I lay her on the bed, I leaned over and kissed her neck tenderly. It elicited a giggle from her gorgeous lips. Her hands slid under my shirt and explored every inch of my back. As I unbuttoned her blouse, I slowly traced kisses along her skin. She reveled in the warmth of my lips against her cold skin as she slid my shirt off while I moved down her body, kiss after kiss to it.

"I've missed this," she purred and ran her fingers through my hair.

I softly kissed her stomach as I slid my hand under her miniskirt and pulled down her pink panties with Hello Kitty on them. She helped me get them off by lifting her legs, then pulled me up into a deep kiss. As she did, her hands fumbled at unbuttoning my pants. My hand caressed her inner thigh as her hand found its way into my pants. We both moaned through the kiss.

"I love you," I moaned into her ear, then bit her neck.

She screamed out in pleasure as my fingers rubbed against her gently. Her nails dug into my back while her other hand rubbed against me. I moaned loudly as I released my bite.

"I love you always," she panted.

I fell asleep wrapped up in her, our clothes scattered haphazardly all over the room. When my alarm went off, it felt like I had only just closed my eyes. Untangling myself from her, I sat on the edge of the bed, still exhausted, along with a bit of guilt weighing on me. I hadn't wanted to talk about where I had gone or why I had left, so I had done something else. Glancing back, I stood to get dressed. I needed a shower, but I was too tired and didn't want to be late. The morning was blistering hot already, so I threw on some light clothes and headed out, running to class.

Chapter Four

I was in the middle of a much-needed, but risky, nap on my lunch break. I had fallen asleep under a palm tree when a gentle tap on my shoulder woke me up. Sitting up, I rubbed the sleep from my eyes and squinted at the bright sunlight. The increasingly familiar face of Casey met my eyes.

"Hey," he said with a large smile.

I waved sleepily and lay my head back against the tree.

"How's your day going?" I muttered as I closed my eyes.

"Pretty easy so far. It's a light day for me today," he said and sat down beside me. "Looks like you didn't get much sleep after you left. Who was that? Bodyguard?"

"Who? Oh, Isiak? No, he just lives with me," I said through a yawn.

"Oh. How many people live with you? When's your next class?" he asked.

I went through the people in my head. "Including the maids and butlers, like twenty people. But I hardly see any of them. They stay in their wing of the place. And I had like two hours between classes."

"Butlers? Maids?" Casey blinked.

"Like I said, it's an inherited house. Those people lived there before," I explained as I opened my eyes. "I'm still not used to it myself, if I'm being honest."

"Oh," he said, quieter.

I sighed, realizing I wasn't going to get to go back to sleep.

"So… what was too much to explain?" he pried.

"Huh? Oh. That. I'm not sure I'm awake enough to explain it all very well at the moment. Meet me in the library at six?"

"Promise?"

I held up my pinky. He raised a brow.

"Give me your hand," I said, nudging him.

He slowly lifted it, and I hooked our pinkies together.

"Now the promise is sealed," I said with a sleepy smile.

"What?" he asked as he studied his hand.

"A pinky promise," I said. "Can't be broken. It's a bond between friends. It is as binding as magic."

"Magic?" he repeated skeptically. "You really believe in that?"

"Without a shred of doubt in my mind," I said, looking him straight in the eyes. "And so will you—when we meet again."

My phone alarm went off, signaling it was time to head to class. I groaned and turned it off.

"See you in a few hours," I said as I stood up. He stood up too, and I caught a glimpse of him as he shook his head in disbelief as I turned and left.

As the last test of my day was underway, I got that weird sensation of being watched. The same one that I had when I woke up the other day. My eyes darted around in confusion as I looked for the source of my unease.

"Keep your eyes to yourself," barked my professor from the front of the class.

I reluctantly looked back at my paper, but not before I noticed a raven that sat on a tree outside the window. I turned my head slightly to see if I could see the rave through my peripheral vision. By the time I did, the raven and the feeling were gone. I cursed under my breath. Things were not going to be easy this year, were they?

While I made my way to the library, I was on the lookout for any ravens that flew around. I hadn't ever seen one in the four years I had been out here, yet now I've seen two within days of each other. Both had also come with that creepy feeling of being watched. I made it to the library earlier than I had expected, and it was just as empty as I hoped it would be. The only people I saw were the ancient-looking librarian, who always seemed to be there no matter the hour, and Casey. He smiled at me as I waved. Sitting next to him, I continued to look around. Someone or something had to be following me, but it seemed it was just us.

"Have you happened to notice any ravens around?" I asked.

"Ravens? Why?" he asked.

"No reason," I shrugged. "Just seen a few around lately. I don't think I've ever seen one in my life."

"One of those weird things you're going to tell me about?"

"Probably. Though I don't know if you'll believe me."

"You've seen what I can do," Casey said with a roll of

his eyes.

"That's true. What do you know about vampires?" I whispered.

"Like, the sparkling kind or the emo kind?" Casey asked with a raised brow.

"Neither really. Just in the general sense."

"Well, depending on what I've watched, some can use magic to go into sunlight with rings. Some glow in the sunlight, so they stay out of it. Dracula himself could walk in the sunlight but couldn't cross running water," Casey said.

"I guess there's a lot of stuff about them. Maybe I shouldn't have started that way," I muttered.

"What do vampires have to do with what you're wanting to tell me?"

"Well, you see… Vampires can't go out in the sun. They also can't come inside a house without being invited. But most importantly, they are real."

He looked at me blankly.

"Look, I know it's hard to believe, but werewolves and vampires do exist. That man you saw come and get me the other night? He is a vampire. When you looked into his eyes, how did you feel?" I asked.

"Like a predator was looking straight into my soul," he mumbled, and shivered.

"Try living with them. It's creepy, to be honest. When they don't like you personally, it's even worse."

"How can you live with them? Don't they drink our blood? Wouldn't they drink yours?"

"Well, the maids I spoke of are basically blood donors. They can't drink my blood, though. It's complicated, but they won't touch me. If I'm right about you, they won't be able to touch you either."

"Why wouldn't they be able to do that?" he asked.

"Outside of vampires, the mythological gods like Zeus and Odin, apparently, also exist. I'm fairly sure one of them was your father," I spat out rapidly.

"My father is Zeus or Odin?" yelled Casey.

"Shhh!" came a loud hiss from the old librarian.

"Sorry," said Casey, embarrassed.

"Not them specifically. I don't know who they would be. My father was Ra," I whispered.

"You're lying to me."

"The coach of the surf team. He's a werewolf," I insisted.

"No. Why did you bring me here? To try to trick me? I thought I had an actual friend," Casey said as he got up to walk away.

"Casey!" I called out after him.

"Quiet," hissed the librarian again. "Or I will have to ask you to leave."

I sat there as Casey walked away and lay my head face down on the table. I'm an idiot. Nobody is going to believe that at face value. After a minute, I stood up and headed home. So much for a new friend. On the walk home, I replayed how I could have handled that better. Maybe I should invite them over to see if for themselves. If they'd talk to me again anyway. When I got home, the house was eerily silent. I made my way through the dark house as I turned on the lights and wound my way through to my room. Light spilled out from under the doorway, but no sounds.

I opened the door, and Ash lay on the bed, only in a pair of boxers, with his feet on the floor. I ran up and jumped on top of him.

"Oof," he grunted as I landed.

I showered him with tiny kisses as he wrapped his arms around me.

"You're back late," he said finally when I stopped.

I locked eyes with him, smiling softly. "Sorry, I didn't realize you were back yet."

He grinned back. "I wanted to surprise you both. But nobody was here when I got back."

I jumped off him and looked at my phone worriedly.

"Where would everyone be?" I asked, as I texted Tessa.

The buzzing of the phone told me that her phone was still on the dresser. Ash looked at the phone, and his face fell.

"She could be in trouble," I said and went towards the door.

Ash grabbed me by the shoulder before I even took a step.

"Wherever she is, she is with the other vampires. They aren't here either," he said and turned me around. "Which means we are alone for now."

My gaze ran up his body until I stared into his oceanic eyes that drew me in. There was a hunger in those depths that mirrored my own. He pulled me into a deep kiss as he led me back to the bed. His skin felt on fire as I lay on top of him, his hands sliding beneath my shirt. The kiss was broken as my shirt came off and was thrown to the floor. I traced my finger down his golden torso with a smile, then pushed him onto his back. I kissed down his body, his arousal already evident as I quickly pulled down his boxers. My tongue flicked out teasingly at the tip as my hand wrapped around the rest of him. As my head bobbed, his moans filled the room, so much so that I almost didn't hear the door creak open. I turned to see Tessa looking at us with a sly smile.

The way her shirt clung to her made it obvious she was already worked up. She sauntered towards us, peeling off her clothes piece by piece. Ash sat up and locked eyes on her swaying hips. I put him back in my mouth as she hungrily kissed him, her fingers tangled in my hair. After a moment, she pulled me up gently and kissed me hard. As she did, she straddled him with a soft moan, while Ash lay back down. My tongue traced where they met as she slowly began to ride him. Their moans grew louder and more desperate the faster she went. She pulled me up, kissing me hungrily.

"Yes, yes, yes!" Ash said as Tessa dug her claws into my back.

While kissing deeply, I let out a soft groan of pleasure and used my hand to caress her inner thighs as she slowed her bouncing on him.

"I love you both!" she yelled as she threw her head back.

I bit her neck as her hands found their way between my legs. Tessa and Ash both breathed heavily as I moaned. Time seemed too slow as I looked into Ash's eyes as he sat back up, and I kissed Tessa's neck. He kissed the other side as he wrapped his large arms around us both and grabbed my butt after a hard slap.

Chapter Five

I lay in the middle of them, one arm draped over Ash, who lay on his back, and Tessa behind me, curled up against me. Ash ran his fingers through her hair as I lay on his shoulder.

"I missed this," Tessa sighed contentedly.

Ash grunted his approval as I smiled and said, "How long has it been?"

"Too long," was all Tessa said as she snuggled closer.

It was early, but I fell asleep blissfully, without a worry about what had happened before with Casey… or with Tessa and Isiak. When I woke to my alarm, Tessa was draped over me, but I couldn't see Ash. I slid out from under her carefully, trying not to jostle her. Every time I moved her while she slept, Beka's warning always came back to me: Never touch a sleeping vampire. Even though it had been a year, I was still cautious, mostly for her sake. Also, dying hurt, so I wasn't eager to do that again anytime soon. I dressed quickly and went in search of Ash. I found him outside at the pool, sitting on the edge with his feet in the water, just in his boxers.

"Hi," I said brightly.

"Morning," he smiled.

His dimples had sent shivers down my spine since we were young, and they still did.

"You're up early."

"I couldn't sleep," he shrugged.

35

"Is everything okay?" I asked worriedly.

"I'm fine," he replied with a laugh. "Just got used to not sleeping long."

"If you say so… Are you going to class today?"

He shook his head. "Not today."

I gave him a quick kiss. "Well, I gotta get going, so I'm not late. I should be back a little after noon."

A little smirk from him and a wave, and I was gone. Everything felt right for the first time in a while. Though, you know how that always goes. Trouble isn't ever far from happiness. As soon as I headed away from the gates of the community, I felt eyes on me. Sure enough, above my head flew a raven. As I noticed it, it darted behind buildings and out of sight.

"I've got to catch that thing," I grumbled.

As I looked up into the sky, hoping to catch another glimpse of the bird, I ran into someone and fell back. First, I hit my butt, then back, and then my head. My vision darkened briefly as the pain shot through my skull. I held the back of my head and groaned as I felt wetness.

"I'm so sorry," said the familiar voice of Casey as I looked up.

She stood above me in a black miniskirt, and I quickly looked to the side. She knelt and looked at me.

"Are you okay?" she asked.

"I don't know. Do you have a bloody lip?" I muttered.

She touched her mouth, and the red on her lips smeared.

"I guess so," she said, licking the blood off her finger.

"Then, guess I'm fine," I groaned.

"I should have watched where I was going," she whispered.

"I was looking up into the sky, it was my fault. I think a bird is following me, and I was looking for it."

"A bird? Is this still part of the tricks you were doing with me yesterday?" she asked, narrowing her eyes.

"You literally switch genders. Why is it so hard to believe what I said?" I sighed and pushed myself up.

"Hmm…" she murmured, then gasped, "Your head!"

"What about it?"

"There's so much blood!"

"Well, that explains the lightheadedness," I muttered as the world tilted.

I collapsed backward onto her lap. She scrambled into her purse and pulled out a handkerchief. She quickly folded it, then gently lifted my head, slid it under, and eased me back down."

"I don't think you're okay," she said.

"I don't either. But I've had worse. Sorry about bleeding on you."

"I've had much worse, too," she said and looked away.

"I'm not lying about what I talked to you about," I mumbled. "I would show you, but… I don't feel like dying. It hurts."

"Dying?" she exclaimed. "Have you tried to kill yourself? You shouldn't do that!"

"I have never tried doing that. I promise."

"Good," she said, letting out a slow breath.

"I gotta get to class," I said and tried to sit back up.

She held me down. "Just stay a little longer. Until your head stops bleeding."

"I'm glad you're talking to me," I murmured.

"I… don't have any friends. It's lonely. I wasn't going to, but then here we are."

"Oh," was all I could say.

I sat up quickly, immediately regretted it, and pressed the kerchief against my head as I staggered to my feet.

"Wait," she called after me.

"I'll be fine. We should go get a burger this weekend. To celebrate my graduation… and your summer," I called over my shoulder.

"Okay!"

I stopped mid-step and turned around. She looked at me, surprised.

"Numbers," I said with a laugh. "We need to exchange them."

She blushed and fumbled for her phone. After exchanging numbers, I handed back the now bloodstained kerchief and promised I'd be okay. Then I ran off, barely making it to class in time. I came home ready to make dinner and enjoy a great movie night.

"What do we want to eat for movie night?" I called as I burst into our room.

Tessa was just sitting in bed, her hair wild from sleep.

"Hmm? Oh." She rubbed her eyes. "I could go for something simple."

"Simple? Simple is good," I agreed while I stripped out of what I had worn to school and put on something comfier.

When I glanced back, she was watching me with a sly grin.

"Course," she purred, "if you just wanted to stay naked, I wouldn't mind just looking at that instead, and we could get delivery."

"Maybe," I teased and jumped onto the bed beside her.

I pushed her hair behind her ear and kissed her forehead, then nose, and finally her lips. She pushed me onto my back and deepened the kiss, lingering there for a long, wonderful minute.

"Go see what Ash wants while I go get what I need," she smiled. "I'll see you soon."

"Do you know where he is?"

She paused, her gaze turning sharp. "By the pool."

"Righty." I stole another kiss. "I will make sure it's something amazing and simple."

She was gone in a blink, leaving me alone on the bed for a moment. I headed out to the side yard, where I found Ash sitting on the pool's edge, feet dangling in the water.

"I'm surprised you aren't swimming," I said as I walked up.

He flinched slightly before twisting to look at me.

"I was earlier," he said with a smile. "Didn't know you were home yet."

I raised a brow. "I was wondering what you would like for dinner. And if you have a movie suggestion, we can put it into a hat to decide."

He shrugged. "I actually just ate. I also think I'm going to turn in early tonight, so the movie doesn't matter to me."

I tilted my head. "Are you okay?"

"Peachy."

He stood and pulled me into a soft hug, and kissed me. Then he left me there, wondering what he wasn't telling me. There had to be something, because he usually lived for my cooking. I couldn't tell if he was lying, something I could always do. Or at least when he was not telling me the full truth. I went to the kitchen to see what I could find that would be easy and also tasty. As I looked through the large walk-in fridge, there was an unsliced log of mortadella. Seeing that made me think of Anthony Bourdain, and I searched the pantry for sourdough bread loaves. Once I found those, I cut out four slices, sliced up a pound of the mortadella, and grabbed slices of provolone cheese I had recently cut. Next, I got out mayo and Dijon mustard from the fridge as my lightly oiled pan heated up on the stove. When I came back, I put half of the mortadella into the pan. I let it brown for a few minutes before I flipped it over. Once I did, I put two slices of the provolone on the meat and put a lid on to let the cheese melt.

After a few minutes, once the cheese was nice and melted, I took it out of the pan and onto a plate. I let the butter melt in the pan, then placed two slices of the bread in it. When the first side toasted, I turned it over and spread Dijon mustard on one slice and mayo on the other. I added the meat to the mayo side and placed the mustard side on top.

40

I put the lid back on and let it cook for another minute, then repeated the process for the second sandwich. I was setting it all up for two when Tessa came in.

"Not finished yet?" she asked, seeing the two plates.

"Ash didn't want one. He said he was going to bed early too, so guess it's just us for the movie," I sighed.

"Is he sick?" she asked worriedly.

"No. At least he didn't seem so. I guess he just needs time to readjust after being back."

"Maybe," she said with a furrowed brow.

"Do you think it's something more?" I asked.

She just shrugged and sat down at the table. The next few days passed without much else happening. Everything was quieter than usual, which I assumed was because Ash had come back. Friday went long, so it was well after dark by the time I came back. The house was dark, which was unusual because the maids and butlers were always moving around. I turned the light on in the foyer when I entered, looking around. There were no sounds of people moving, and no lights visible in the further reaches of the house. I floundered my way to the next light switch, heading towards the kitchen. That was when I heard voices and saw light spilling from under the doorway.

"You did what?" yelled Tessa.

"I sent away the vampires," Ash said nonchalantly.

"Why? How? Who gave you the right?" Tessa growled with a mix of anger and pain.

Chapter Six

As I made my way slowly towards the voices, there was a heartbeat of silence when Tessa spoke again, "Why?"

"They wanted to leave, we couldn't just keep them here," replied Ash.

"Do you have any idea what they're going to do? They've been invited in. And all the maids and butlers? Where is Keira?" asked Tessa, her voice was calm with the undertone of holding back an explosion.

"That is what I would like to know, too," chimed in Corri. "While I am okay with the others who have gone on their way, our livestock is still needed."

"They shouldn't be slaves to your kind," growled Ash.

"You, young boy, don't belong here either," Isiak snapped. "They are given all amenities these days. Back when I was turned, we used to hang them in cellars."

As I stood dumbfounded in the hall, the door burst open as Tessa ran out. As she went by me, I put my arm out and wrapped it around her. She turned to me, and her eyes were bloodshot, bright purple, filled with rage and heartbreak. Even in the dark hall, they glowed bright enough to see them clearly. Her body went limp against mine as I held her there. I didn't say anything, I had no words that would help as I held her tightly. Her body heaving as she cried into my chest.

"Let's not fight," came Corri's voice from the room.

Apparently, the conversation wasn't over even without

Tessa there.

"One thing is right: if those who decided to leave end up going to the other side, we will be in trouble again. We should make sure we lock up things tightly and block the secret passages," Isiak warned.

"You two should leave, too. Why do you stay?" asked Ash.

"This is my house. I don't give up my things so easily," retorted Isiak.

"Why we stay doesn't matter," interjected Corri simultaneously.

"Whatever. I will make sure everything is tightened up. I don't trust you," Ash muttered.

I heard him stomp off in a different direction from where I stood with Tessa. I heard the footsteps of Corri and Isiak heading in a third direction. When they were gone, Tessa pushed herself off me and turned on the light in the hall we stood in. Her face was paler than usual, and her normal ruby lips were a dull pink.

"Are you okay?" I asked. "Besides, whatever that was in there?"

"I… haven't eaten yet," she muttered. "I don't have anything to."

"Did Keira actually leave?" I asked.

She shrugged slightly and looked at the ground. I took out my phone and texted Keira to wait for a reply. We sat in the hall waiting for a reply when a low rumble escaped Tessa's lips.

"I need to go, I can't wait," she growled softly. "I've

only been eating once a night, and I've gone over twenty-four hours since I last fed."

Her normally white sclera was red.

"Will it be safe?" I asked.

She stood and turned away, then was gone without a sound. My head dropped between my legs, and my arms hung over my knees. Even if I had wanted to, I couldn't have stopped her. I needed to work up the courage to talk to Ash, to figure out what was going on in that thick skull of his. Still unsure of what to say to him, I stood up to make myself a simple roasted turkey sandwich. After I finished the sandwich, I went looking for him. Unsurprisingly, I found him at the side of the pool. This time, he was soaking in the moonlight as he lay on the lounge chair.

"Hi," I breathed.

He jumped, startled, and sat up.

"Oh, hi," he replied.

"Why?" I asked.

"Why what?"

"Why did you send everyone away?"

"They wanted to go. I just gave them permission from the top dog of this group," he answered.

"It's something we should have discussed. You wanted Tessa to take care of what the vampires did not even two weeks ago."

"Then I saw nothing was being taken care of. Those creatures were going to do worse than leave. Everyone was gone, so I chose to do something about it."

"How did you get the others to leave before Tessa woke?" I questioned.

"The humans, I had leave mid-afternoon. The vampires, well, I had a talk with them the night before. They left an hour before sunrise. Except those two, they just won't go."

"I think Isiak actually cares about Tessa, in his own weird way. Which just means he still thinks he owns her like he does this house," I muttered. "There's no way he would have agreed to his vampires leaving. How did you make him side with you?"

"Easy. I said I'd allow him to stay and not throw him out into the sunlight while he slept."

I stood there with my mouth agape. I couldn't fathom Ash doing this, yet here he was. My best friend, since I could remember, had changed more than I had thought since becoming the Alpha. I didn't see Tessa the rest of that night, and I slept in a spare room to stay away from Ash.

I woke up to a few texts from Casey. The first one asked how the finals went. Next asked when I wanted to meet. The last said they were free in the afternoon. I texted back that one in the afternoon for a late lunch would be nice. A second later, they said that would be good. With a couple of hours to kill, I got up to get a shower. As I was lathering up, I heard the door open.

"Hello?" I called, my eyes closed.

"Hi," came a reply from Ash in a husky voice.

I heard the shower door open as I washed the soap off my face.

"I'm not in the mood," I muttered as he stepped in next

to me.

"Oh, come on," he murmured, wrapping his arms around me. "It's just us right now."

I pulled away from him and turned around. "No."

I got out still a little soapy and didn't even dry off as I walked through the house naked. It was just me anyway, since all the other humans had left. At least so I had been told. I was incredibly surprised when I turned a corner and saw Keira standing at the door to my room. She turned towards me as I came around the corner.

"Uh…" I stammered, dumbfounded.

"Ack!" she yelped and spun away.

"Sorry, sorry. Let me through quickly," I said as I used my hands to cover myself as best that I could.

"Why are you walking around naked?" she scolded through the door.

"Why are you here?" I countered.

"I live here."

"Didn't you leave?" I asked as I came out in a robe.

"No."

"But you weren't here the other day."

"I got called away by one of my foster sisters. She needed help. It took longer than I thought. I told Ash," she replied with a raised brow. "Where is everyone else? The rooms are empty."

"They all left."

"What? Why?"

46

"Ash said they wanted to leave. Everyone except Isiak, Corri, me, Tessa, and Ash."

"Why would we want to do that?" Keira asked, confused.

She rubbed her arm and shrank into herself.

"I'm not sure," I admitted. "What's wrong?"

"I… I just have nowhere else to go. And I know a lot of the other girls didn't either. This was the best that we had."

"You can stay. And if someone tells you otherwise, come tell me. I will make sure they know that I'm the one who said you could stay."

"If you say so," she whispered, like she didn't believe what I said.

"I know you're new here, but I am the leader of my faction in this area. I'm not human."

"You aren't?" she gasped. "I just thought…"

"Thought that I was just here for eye candy?" I laughed. "I know I'm not much to look at, but believe you me, nobody in this place would ever lay a scratch on me."

"What… are you?" she asked.

"I'm… not sure. It sounds too pretentious to say, 'a god', but I don't know what else to call it."

She scoffed.

"I'm serious," I pouted. "I'm not human. Don't know what I should be called."

"Okay," she said.

"Look, you can stay. Do what you do. I will make sure that Tessa knows you're back. She can explain things to you."

There seemed to be a lot of things I needed to speak with Tessa about.

"What should I do?" Keira asked.

"What do you mean?"

"Well, I usually just help out the others with little tasks. But nobody is here."

"Just… take the day to yourself. Take a dip in the pool. Take a long shower. Fix yourself something to eat," I shrugged. "I am going to be out for a few. Just stay away from Ash."

"Why?" she asked.

"Just… I don't know. Just do it, please."

"Fine," she said.

I went back into my room to get dressed to hang out with Casey. I didn't want to be in the house any longer, so I left for the diner hours early.

Chapter Seven

I sat in the leather booth reading a book while I waited for Casey to show. She came in early and was surprised to see me there.

"Why are you here so early?" she asked as she sat next to me.

"I just wanted to be out of the house, and I had nothing else to do," I lied.

She cocked her head to the side but didn't say anything.

"So, did your finals go well?" I asked.

"I hope so. I need to pass with at least a B in all my classes if I want to keep my scholarship. I've been so stressed all week."

"I'm sure you did fine," I said, bumping her shoulder, "Hope you have a major you're working towards. I've... mostly given up on what I was going there for, but I will have a BA. So, if I ever need it, I'll have that going for me."

"What were you originally going there to do?" she asked.

"I was going to continue on and go for archaeology. But I've had my fill of learning about things from the past. Still, my degree will be a BA in history."

"What made you give up on your dream?" she looked concerned.

"Oh, meeting people from it," I said with a shrug.

"When you know someone from over a thousand years ago, it doesn't feel like ancient history."

She let out a deep sigh and turned towards the menu.

"Look, something bad happened at home. It involves the things I told you. There might be a lot of terrible creatures out in the dark. You might be safe, at least if you're what I believe you to be. Roommates or anyone else you know, however, might not be," I whispered.

"What do you mean?"

"There were a lot of vampires that left my house, and I don't know where they will go," I said, with a hint of fear creeping through my voice.

"Did you forget to take meds?" Casey asked and scooted slightly away.

I sighed, "Casey, I'm not lying. People like you, people who have abilities like you, and me... we aren't food or prey to the creatures of the night. Well, most of the creatures of the night. Our blood is deadly to them, and they will not attack us. If you know anyone normal, though, they could be in danger."

"Say I do believe you; I don't have any friends around here. The only other people I know are in the same school as we are. Why haven't you warned them?"

"The people I know in the school are werewolves. They're not exactly in trouble of being attacked."

"I will keep my eyes out for bats," she said.

"I don't think they can turn into those," I mumbled.

"It was a joke."

"I'm not joking," I said. "Just… be safe at night. Try to stay inside if possible. That's one thing that is true about legends."

"Fine. Can we talk about anything else?"

"Okay, okay. So, what are you going to major in?" I asked.

"Engineering. I might try to get a master's in it. Though who knows how well that will go."

"Oh, I got a future rocket scientist next to me, huh?"

"Not that kind. I just want to be able to understand and engineer something that could help the world out. Something that can help people who really need it," she said with a shrug.

I nudged her with my shoulder, "I'll be around to try to help you out. Just not with the math. Or the building. Or anything that isn't supportive of a friend."

She laughed and shook her head. Time passed by too quickly. When I saw her eyes start looking like they were struggling to stay open, I decided it was time for me to say goodnight.

"Want me to walk you home?" I asked when we left the diner.

"I'll be fine," she yawned. "The dorms aren't too far away."

I shrugged. "Well, go get some rest. I'll probably do the same."

I watched her walk off and turned the opposite way. I debated going back home, but I decided to take a walk instead. It was late, but I also knew I wasn't in any danger.

There was a small park a few blocks from the diner I had only seen in passing, but I knew it had no fence and a few swings. So, it sounded like the perfect place. Something caused me to look up, a feeling or maybe just chance, but when I did, a bird darker than the night sky was flying off.

"I almost miss the days before I came to this town," I sighed as I put my hands in my pockets and headed toward the park.

To my surprise, there were lights in the park, and a couple of taller men were on the basketball court doing a one-on-one. As I passed them, they stopped mid-game and stared at me. I kept my head down and made my way to the swings. They didn't make my skin crawl, so I just thought they were normal people, paid them no attention, and hoped they didn't try to cause me trouble. Dying wasn't something I cared about doing tonight. Once I sat on a swing, they started playing ball again as if I weren't there. From the swings, I was able to look to my left and see the two. As I watched them go back and forth, point for point, I lost track of time and didn't even think of my problems. It didn't hurt that their shirtless physiques were also easy on the eyes. Covered in sweat, skilled at a sport I could never hope to be, and athletic… I seemed to have a type. However, I think most people had that same type.

My thoughts were interrupted as my phone rang. I pulled it out and saw it was Casey.

"Missing me already," I laughed.

"Someone is following me," he said in a whisper. "I'm scared."

"What? What's going on? Where are you?" I asked.

"Shouldn't you have been home already?"

"I heard something following me and didn't want to lead whoever it was to my place. I hid in an alley behind a dumpster, but I know they're nearby," he whispered. "Can you come?"

"Where are you?" I asked.

There was a blood-curdling scream... then the phone went silent. A moment later, I noticed a text from Casey with his location pinned. I didn't hesitate. I just started running, praying I wasn't too late. Deep down, however, I knew I could never make it those few miles on foot before whoever, or whatever, had followed him could hurt, if not kill, him. Almost twenty minutes later, I arrived at his pinned location. It was an alley with no streetlamps anywhere. It was complete darkness, even where I stood at the entrance. I stood there, too scared to move into the pitch blackness. My mind raced with images of what I would find. A mangled body, only a piece of his body, just slumped against a wall, dead. Whatever I found down there, I knew it would be two bodies. Unless, of course, it had been a vampire, since a true scion would probably dust them like I did.

I forced myself to take a few deep breaths to calm my nerves and push the gruesome thoughts out of my head. Then I walked cautiously down the alley. I didn't use my phone light because I didn't want to see the gore in the illumination. Whatever I saw, it would be better as vague shapes. I passed small bins until eventually I came to the edge of a large dumpster that looked big enough to hide Cazimir inside. I stopped with my hand on the edge I had been walking toward and let out a breath I hadn't realized I had been holding in. Slowly, I made my way along the dumpster to the other side, and when I peered around it, something slammed into my face. I felt my nose break as I stumbled back. I hit the wall and slid down it, fell onto my butt, and let my legs go straight out. What good was being unable to die, and being able to revive without scars, if I had to deal with broken bones like a normal person? Being a god sucks and makes no sense.

"Get away from me!" yelled Casey.

"It's me," I choked out.

"Rai?" he asked.

I turned on my phone's flashlight as I held my head back to keep the blood from flowing even more down my face. He gasped and then hugged me.

"I am so sorry! I thought you were that thing that followed me," he said in relief.

He pulled back, "Oh my god! You're bleeding!"

He jumped up and searched his pockets frantically.

"I picked a fine time to not have my purse," he grumbled.

"It's fine," I said as I used the wall to help me stand up. "What was it that followed you?"

"I… I can't explain it," he whispered.

"Was it a large wolf? Though the moon's not right," I muttered as I looked into the sky.

"No. I have no idea what it was. I heard someone follow me. That's why I called you. It then came around the corner the same way you did, but I was able to see these red eyes. They were enormous. I screamed, threw my phone at it, and turned away. Next thing I knew, I heard the sound of beating wings. I looked up and saw a dark figure fly the way you came down from. I stayed where I was, thinking it was waiting for me to come out, and then got tired of waiting."

"What do you mean by enormous red eyes?"

"I mean that the eyes were bulbous and the size of my hand. They were an oval shape and came out of its head."

"That's… new. Let's get you home," I said.

"I have a first aid kit there as well."

"That will be nice," I said and lowered my head.

The dorms were a few blocks away, back towards the direction I had come from, so it didn't take long to get there. His roommate had left for the summer, back to some town he didn't know. But they had left right after classes earlier that day, so we were alone.

"So, um, welcome to my humble abode," Casey said with a blush as he opened the door.

He showed me to the bathroom. As I washed the blood off my face and neck, I heard him throwing things around to straighten up his side of the room. Out of breath, he appeared at the doorway and leaned against the doorframe.

"So, your roommate doesn't mind how you change?" I asked.

"I'm lucky if she even realizes I'm real. She's hardly ever around; when she is, she's asleep, snoring loudly, or stoned out of her mind. Otherwise, she is out, doing something that involves… animal skulls."

I looked at myself in the bathroom mirror and sighed as I looked at my shirt. It was covered in blood.

"I would lend you a shirt, but I don't know if it would fit," offered Casey. "I could wash it for you in the downstairs washer."

"It's okay. I'll just need to avoid most of the people I live with until I get to my room."

"So… they're actually vampires?"

"And a werewolf. Also, a few humans."

"I find this all hard to believe to be true. But what I saw… that thing was not human."

"Whatever it was, I'm guessing it left you alone because you're a scion, or demi-god, or whatever you want to call it. Or something more," I said.

"There is no shot my father was a god. Why would he leave me alone in this cold, cruel world?"

"From what I gather, it's what they do," I growled. "That's why I'm never having kids. It's like gods are predisposed to just abandon every offspring they have with humans."

She stared at me.

"Sorry. It's a sore subject," I muttered.

"You're not a god. You'd never be like them," she said, placing a hand on my shoulder.

I sighed but nodded my head, not wanting to argue that I was. I didn't notice her move closer until her face was inches from mine.

"You came to save me. Nobody has ever been there for me like that," she whispered.

Her hand slid down my arm. I followed it with my eyes

56

as her fingers laced with mine. I looked up, my mouth slightly open—then her lips pressed against mine.

Chapter Eight

As her tongue flicked against mine, I stumbled back to get away, but she came with me. I landed hard on the floor with her on top of me. When her hand went under my shirt and started traveling up my body, I pushed her off me.

"I can't do this," I said and stood up.

"I'm sorry," she said as she knelt on the floor and looked down.

I left the dorm as fast as I could. As soon as I was outside the building, I ran all the way home. The place was unlit except for the maid's quarters. I turned on every light as I made my way through the maze to the room I shared with Tessa and Ash. As I approached the door, I heard yelling.

"No! You had no right to tell my people to leave!" yelled Tessa.

"I'm the man of this castle. I can do whatever I want, and think is right," growled Ash.

"The only thing you're the 'man' of is that pack of dogs you chased away!"

There was a loud thwack sound, followed almost at once by a loud thud from across the room. I threw open the door to see Tessa face down on the other side of the room by the far wall. Ash stood with his arms crossed and his back to me.

"Ash! What did you do!?" I yelled.

He turned to face me with an unnatural anger in his

bright blue eyes and a sneer on his face. I rushed past him, and he grabbed me by the collar of my shirt. With almost no effort, he flung me out through the open doorway.

"Go away," he growled. "This is between me and the dead thing over there."

As I stood back up, I saw Tessa staring at Ash from the ground where she was still lying. The look of betrayal and heartbreak in her eyes shattered something inside me. I blinked, and Tessa was gone. A loud, robust laugh had me look around in confusion. Who could feel joy in this cold, dark world? I looked at Ash and saw his shoulders rising and falling. Was he crying? Did he realize he went too far? Then it hit me. The sound of laughter was coming from him.

"What the hell is wrong with you?" I snapped.

"Oh? You're still here? I was thinking, this is a nice house to have for myself. The dead freaks are gone. That 'maid' I missed is packing up to leave as we speak. Now you need to leave also," Ash said nonchalantly.

"Leave? To where? I own this house!"

He pulled his pants down, and a stream of urine splattered the doorway that separated us.

"And now I've marked it as my territory," he said with a slight smirk.

I didn't know what to say as I stood there with my mouth agape. Finally, I turned around to find Keira. I couldn't fathom what had happened to Ash while he had been away, but I knew how to find out. I found Keira as she was coming out of her room, a couple of suitcases in hand.

"Oh, thank God you're still alive," said Keira. "Maybe

you can talk some sense into Ash."

"I don't think I can. I do know someone who can, though, and I need you to drive me to the airport so I can go home."

"Aren't we in your home?" she asked, puzzled.

"Back to where I come from, where me and Ash grew up," I said. "I need a ride to the airport so I can go see what happened to him while he was gone."

"What about Tessa?"

"I need you to find her and help her through this."

"You know she would prefer it to be you."

"I can't be there for her right now… Not if I want to figure out what happened to Ash. That and next time I see her, I have to tell her something that is better discussed when whatever is happening is over," I sighed wearily.

She glanced at me, then we drove the rest of the way to the airport in silence.

"Find Tessa and keep her safe and sane, please," I said when Keira dropped me off.

"I'll do my best," was all she said.

The next plane that left was a couple of hours later, so I made my way through security to the gate and took a small nap. Or at least that was the plan. I couldn't get what I had seen out of my head. The look on Tessa's face, the way Ash talked, it was all too much to take. And then there was Casey. That was not something I looked forward to dealing with when the time came. I finally closed my eyes when I heard my flight's call for boarding. Soon, I was in the sky and finally asleep for the next five hours. After a few hours in Atlanta, I was on the last couple of hours to my final destination.

It was almost noon by the time I made it off the plane and to the rent-a-car service. It was another three hours before I was in familiar territory. I passed by my old high school and felt almost bad. I didn't even miss it in the slightest. No matter what happened in the last year, it was still the best year of my life, until the last few days. I stopped a block from my parents' house. I hadn't seen them in a while and needed to prepare myself mentally. Like I have said, they're still the strangest thing about my life. A couple of minutes later, I pulled up to a two-bedroom single-story house that sat on an acre of land. It sat at the back of the property, had a wraparound porch with two rocking chairs on either side of the front door. The house was old and brick, dating back to the early 1800s.

I drove down the dirt lane and wondered if they would even be home. Wouldn't be the first time I came to visit, and they would be off locked around some trees. At those times, they even knew I was coming to visit them. As usual, I walked up to the house and found the door unlocked.

"Hey, Mom! I'm home!" I yelled as I opened the door.

From the kitchen, I heard rustling sounds, and I made my way there. Throwing open drawers was my mother. Tall, thin, long black beehive hair, just like when I last saw her.

"Mom? Hello?" I said.

She stopped and turned towards me. Her brown eyes grew wide, and a big, toothy grin spread across her face.

"Oh, my little Rai of sunshine," she said, wrapping me in a tight hug.

I hugged back just as tightly as I cringed, "Stop calling

me that."

"Never," she said with a laugh.

She leaned back and held me by the shoulders.

"Have you gotten taller? How long has it been? A week? Two?" she asked.

"Two years."

"Can't be. How was college all that time?"

"Well, I've graduated from that now. Thought I would come say hello," I lied.

"Your dad will be so happy when he gets home."

"Where is he?"

"Oh, locked down at the city courthouse."

'What is he doing there?"

"Oh, same old thing," she said with a wave of her hand.

"How long is he going to be there?"

"Oh, he should be home today. I think. Oh, right, I came to find the key. I misplaced it somewhere."

I shook my head. "You mean the key that is around your neck?"

She felt her neck and pulled up a necklace with a small key.

"Oh, right. I left it there so I wouldn't lose it. I guess I didn't need to come home after all," she said with a small laugh. "Let's go get your dad."

"Fine," I laughed.

My parents' car was an old, beat-up truck that was older than they were. It also had no AC. So, we drove fifteen miles to town in triple-digit weather and open windows. Nothing had changed in the last twenty-two years. The courthouse was on the main road through town, and of course, only my dad was around. He had chained himself up to the front door of the place, though in a way that let people enter as they wished.

Chapter Nine

"Hey, Dad," I said as I walked up.

He was a tiny, bald man. His beard was almost a foot long.

"Oh, my little light Rai," my father said, his gray eyes lighting up as he saw me.

I facepalmed, "Don't you start either. Can we just go home?"

"Is it dinnertime already? What are we having? I might want to stay another day," he said.

"Well, I was thinking we could go to Mama Jack's. Though we could let Mom cook something up," I said with a shrug.

"Don't let her near my stove. She's liable to burn the house down," he said.

"I am not that bad of a cook," laughed my mother.

"Mom," I said with a smile.

"Okay fine. I might not have picked up such a skill in my lifetime, but I have plenty of other skills," she humphed.

My dad and I both laughed out loud at my mother's pouting face.

"Still here I see, Marcus," said Judge Kenny as he walked out the door.

"Might be going home today, Kenny. My child is home," said my dad.

"Oh? Hey there, Rai. Have you liked it in that big city?" Judge Kenny asked as he noticed me.

"Well, it's not that big, sir. It's been nice, though. Me and Ash have had a long few years."

"That Ulfr boy is trouble. Never thought I would see him in college instead of in front of my courtroom."

"He's even going back for another two years. As long as nothing has changed with him in the last few months," I said.

"That's good. That whole family of his is always wild when they're young. Then they become outstanding citizens as adults. Though none have ever left like him," said Judge Kenny. "Now, Marcus, go on and be with your family while Rai is in town."

"Will do, Judge."

Mom unlocked Dad, and we all got back into the truck. After dinner at the local diner, with a ton of questions about what I had been up to, we made it back to the small house. My room hadn't been changed at all. Movie posters, a freshly made bed, and my old desk, where I spent many nights doing homework. It was like nobody had set foot in the room for the last few years. Even my old television was on the wall. My parents had never watched television that I knew of, so when they bought me my own, I had been ecstatic. Ash's house was where we watched most movies as kids. Except for the nights he would sneak over, and we would watch something scary in my room after my parents were asleep.

Like clockwork, my parents were in bed before nine. They'd wake up with the rising sun, and one of them would work on the garden while the other would see something in the morning paper, and they'd go be a one-person advocate against it. The townspeople put up with them. Heck, when we'd have cookouts, most of the town would come. My parents were just the weird friends that one had and went to see every Memorial Day, or any other day that had a cookout. My mom might not know how to cook, but my dad was a wiz on his grill.

I lay in my bed, thinking about what I would have to do while I was here. If something had happened to Ash, it would have happened here. I was scared that his parents had also been changed by something. As I lay there, my phone rang.

"Hey, Casey," I answered.

"I'm so sorry about the other night," he said.

"It's fine. I just, I can't do that," I muttered.

"I thought there was more between us," he said.

"It's… I'm married."

"What? I never saw any rings?"

"It's complicated, Casey. I'll explain everything when I get back."

"Back? Where did you go? I didn't chase you off, did I?"

"No, I'm visiting my parents. It's nothing… honestly."

"Are you sure?" he asked.

"Of course. When I got home, things just got really strange, and I needed to come back for a few days," I said with half-truths.

"What do I do if I see that thing again?"

"You should be fine, honestly. Things like that shouldn't bother you at all. If you need anything, though, just call me."

"If you say so."

I could tell something was wrong, but I didn't feel like pushing it, so I just said bye and hung up the phone. I already had enough to deal with. Tessa hadn't answered any of my texts, and neither had Keira. The next morning, we returned the rental car because my parents didn't want me to pay for it while I was staying. One night turned into days as I stuck around. I helped my parents around the house, cooked for them, and kept myself busy in general.

"How long are you going to be staying?" Dad asked one night at dinner.

"Not too much longer," I said, half lying, since I didn't know when I would get the courage to go to the Ulfr household.

I woke up the next morning to the smell of burnt coffee.

"Mom?" I asked.

I made my way to the kitchen as I rubbed the sleep from my eyes.

"Ugh, I can never get this thing to work right. Why did we ever buy this electric thing?" Mom grumbled.

"What did you do?" I asked with a laugh.

"I don't know. Your father usually makes the coffee, but he was gone when I woke up this morning."

The front door swung open.

"I'm home," came Dad's voice.

"Speak of the devil," Mom said.

"Help me out, Rai. I have meat that needs to be

marinated," Dad said as he came in carrying a few racks of ribs.

"Expecting a party?" I asked with a raised brow.

"Of course. Though I had planned on less, Ash invited his family over tomorrow night to celebrate graduation."

"You saw Ash? He's here?" I asked, my eyes going wide.

"I don't think that boy has left this town in years," said Dad.

"Wait, you've seen him a lot?"

"Maybe. What is a lot? He would always bring great jerky treats to me while I was in front of the courthouse."

I stood there, unable to process what I heard. I mean, my parents aren't the most dependable when it comes to giving actual time frames, unless they're trying to be serious. But I also couldn't press them without making them worried. I was not about to tell them that the family friends were werewolves. Ash must have followed me home. The biggest question was why. He got what he wanted when I left the house.

"Rai? Are you going to help me, or am I going to have to do all this alone? I think Ulric and Lyra are also bringing Jane and John," said Dad as he brought me out of my thoughts. "Those kids have an appetite worse than Ash did."

"Yea, yea. All the spices in the same place?" I asked.

"Of course."

"I will go clean up the yard," Mom said.

I cleared the kitchen table while Dad cleared the counter. We took out the large cutting boards, and between us were eighteen full racks of ribs. With spices spread around the sides of the cutting board, I started to prep the marinade for my side. In a large bowl, I poured half a cup of soy sauce, followed by a quarter cup of apple cider vinegar. A heaping tablespoon of honey followed next. After that, I reached for the knives, followed by garlic. With an ease that comes from years of practice, I peeled and minced a half dozen cloves. After I tossed those into the bowl, I grated a tablespoon of ginger into it.

Next up was a handful of finely sliced green onions. A half teaspoon of ground cinnamon, a dash of black pepper, a pinch of salt, and some freshly grated nutmeg finished it off. As I mixed the marinade together with a wooden spoon, I poured a cup of whiskey in, then a dash of toasted sesame oil. As the flavors blended together, the smell made my mouth water. Behind me, my dad hummed as he worked, adding his own blend of spices. When I was done making the marinade, it was time to score the ribs. I made shallow cuts into the meat so that the marinade would penetrate it and make it more flavorful inside and out.

Once done, I placed the ribs in the marinade and massaged it into the meat, ensuring every inch was evenly coated. I lost track of time until I was satisfied with the result, then sealed the bowl with plastic wrap to place it in the refrigerator. Then I repeated the process eight more times. My dad watched me with pride in his eyes as I put the last of the marinating ribs into the fridge until tomorrow morning. It was almost like a contest between us, and the Ulfr's would decide who had the best marinade. Though I also knew that the majority of them wouldn't even taste the flavor as they wolfed down the meat.

"Are you two done?" Mom asked as she came inside.

She was covered in dirt, and her hair was sticking out in places.

"I think so. Um, need me to go help in the yard?" I asked.

"No, no. I was just in the garden. We will even have some vegetables for dinner tomorrow. Though the Ulfr's never eat them."

"Hey, I've gotten Ash to eat some while we've been out in SoCal," I said with a laugh.

"Oh, what a miracle you've worked with that boy, then," Mom said with a grin.

"I try."

I tried not to think about Ash for the rest of the day, but it didn't work. He was the only thing on my mind, and if he wasn't, it was Tessa. I hoped she was okay, and that Keira had found her. That she wasn't answering me worried me more every day. I went outside to sit on the porch, and the first thing I noticed was a raven sitting on the top of my parents' truck.

"What are you?" I murmured.

As my mom came out, the raven took flight.

"What was that?" she asked.

"Just a raven," I said with a shrug.

"Oh? That thing has been hanging around here for the last few days," she said. "Usually, they try to go for my garden, but this one is a strange one."

"Really? I hadn't seen it since I got here."

"Oh, it definitely has been. I almost feel like it follows me. That's just crazy talk, though. Birds don't follow people," she said.

"How do you know it's the same bird?" I asked.

"Well, isn't it obvious?" Mom asked.

"No," I muttered.

"The eyes. Never seen one with a pure silver eye."

As I stared at it, it turned to stare back at me. That was when I noticed it, one eye was as dark as its feathers, and the other looked like mercury.

"Weird," I whispered.

"That's nature for you. So many things seem weird and unexplainable."

"What if there was something that was simply unexplainable?"

"No such thing. Everything has an answer."

"If you say so, Mom."

She looked me straight in the eyes. "You might not like the answer. The answer might not even satisfy you when you learn it. The answer is still an answer, no matter how it makes you feel."

"I get it."

"Do you? I know you're not here just to see us."

I pulled my gaze away from her.

"I don't expect you to tell us whatever you're going through, but if you decide to, we will understand."

"It's nothing to worry about," I mumbled.

She kissed the top of my head. "Rai Eckles, I have worried about you nonstop for twenty-two years. I will continue to do so for as long as I live. It's what you do as a parent who loves their child."

"Love you too, Mom," I said as I looked back up at her.

Chapter Ten

It was almost noon when I woke up. Nobody was in the house as I came out of my room. I found Dad preheating his prize smoker, and Mom was in her garden.

"Need any help, Mom?" I asked.

"Of course. We have a lot to do, and you've slept the entire day away."

"Sorry. I couldn't get to sleep last night. That raven kept tapping on my window," I yawned.

"Oh, that was that noise. I had such a weird dream—something was knocking outside my door. When I opened it, there was this frail old woman, and when I touched her… she turned to dust. It was strange," said Mom.

"Did… she look familiar? Any features stick out?" I asked.

"Oh, I don't know. All details faded—you know how that is."

I nodded. I spent the next hour helping Mom pick fresh vegetables, mostly red and green cabbages, potatoes, and carrots. As Dad loaded the ribs into the smoker, I made thin slices of the cabbage and grated the carrots into a bowl to start the coleslaw, while Mom mashed some of the potatoes. The remaining potatoes would be used to make potato wedges. Once I was done with the veggies, I grabbed some mayo, Dijon mustard, apple cider vinegar, maple syrup, and celery seeds to whip together the coleslaw dressing. After tasting, I added salt and pepper and adjusted the ingredients to ensure perfection. I then mixed the dressing with the carrots and cabbage and placed it in the fridge to chill.

As Mom cut the rest of the potatoes into wedges for me to deep-fry, I began with the barbecue sauce. Dad came in to help as well. He was going to make his own special sauce for his ribs, just to keep the unofficial taste test fair. One day, he'd tell me what he used, or so he always claimed.

I started with three cups of ketchup, and brown sugar, a cup of red wine vinegar, and water, two tablespoons of Worcestershire sauce and dry mustard, four teaspoons of paprika, salt, and black pepper, and a generous amount of hot sauce into a hot pot. As I stirred and tasted, I added a little more pepper and brown sugar before bringing it to a boil. To keep his sauce a secret, my dad took random ingredients that may or may not have actually been in his recipe and made it out on the back porch.

That little bit of time was a lifesaver. It gave me something else to focus on instead of Ash getting closer to being in my house. In the next couple of hours after that, with nothing to do except wait to cook the potatoes, I decided to take a long walk into the woods. I knew them like the back of my hand, and it was nice to see them again. Though being in them just made me think of how the Ulfr's used these same woods when changed into wolves. Which, I guess, is why our little town was rumored to have the biggest wolf population in the state. Some people even claimed they had seen Bigfoot in their backyards. I wondered if they genuinely had, or if what they saw were the Ulfr's.

Once everything was over, I would have to ask about that. My head whipped back and forth as I thought about

Bigfoot being real. That was when I saw the same silver-eyed raven sitting in a tree.

"Go away!" I yelled.

It seemed to listen and took off through the tree canopy and into the sky. A few minutes later, I heard the sound of a twig snap.

"I am an idiot. I thought I watched enough horror movies not to do this," I said, whipping my head toward the sound.

"You came to the wrong place," growled a deep, inhuman voice.

Another twig snapped from the opposite direction.

"Look, I'm sorry. You don't want to do this," I pleaded, a tremble in my voice.

"I don't know what you are, but this is our territory, and we don't take kindly to others coming in," came a different, slightly higher-pitched voice.

"I should have thought of that sooner. I live in the house about a mile back. I'm not here to take over or anything," I whimpered as I turned towards the new voice.

"Nobody like you lives there. We would know. Too many strange things have been in our woods lately. We need to clean house," snapped the first voice.

"Wait... I know that voice," I said as something clicked in my head. "I mean, you sound creepier, but I know you. Why can't I place it?"

"I don't think you know me at all. But you soon will."

"Lowell! Dang, you were like sixteen when I left. How

do you not remember me?"

"How do you know my name?" wavered the voice, now sounding more human.

Out from behind a tree stepped a man a few years younger than me. His dark red hair was long, covering his face all the way to his bare chest. He stood almost as tall as Ash, but was much slimmer.

"You idiot, that's Rai," a woman's voice interjected.

From behind me stepped the woman. Her hair was just as wild as his, just brown, and she wore a tattered shirt.

"Raulene? You too? The Fairchilds and the Ulfrs?"

"You know what we are? Do your parents?" asked Raulene sharply.

"Not as far as I know. Why weren't you two at the ceremony last year?"

"Well, the Fairchilds aren't part of the Ulfr's pack. And Lowell over here decided he finally wanted to marry me. After a long discussion, we joined with my pack since my daddy is the leader. What ceremony did the Radiant Moonlight pack go away to?" she asked.

"Not important, I guess, since they didn't tell you. How many werewolf packs are around here?"

"Just two," replied Lowell. "We split these woods in half."

"So, you know what we are... What are you?" asked Raulene.

"What do you know about gods?"

"You mean the one who did that rainbow flood thing?"

76

asked Lowell.

"No. The ones from mythology," I said.

"Nothing. Though I go to church every Sunday," said Lowell.

I shrugged. "Again, not the same thing. But I'm just another oddity in life. One of the great mysteries of this world."

"What about that other thing that's been in my woods?" asked Raulene.

"I don't know of anything else. What have you seen?"

"Ain't seen anything. But the scent… It's nothing I've ever smelled before. Daddy said it isn't vampires, like we couldn't have figured that out without his help. The fact even he doesn't know what it is worries me. He always talks about all sorts of creatures," said Lowell.

"Fantastic," I groaned. "Just what I need in my life, more unanswered questions."

"Don't worry. We will find this thing and take care of it," promised Raulene.

"Just be safe."

"We gonna be fine," replied Lowell.

I nodded and headed home. The last thing I wanted was to be around if they found whatever it was they were looking for. With a howl, I heard them running off deeper into the woods. I got home just in time to start frying the potato wedges. Another welcome distraction from my life. The clock seemed to tick by too fast as I watched it. The ever-approaching hour Ash would arrive.

"You seem nervous," Mom said as I paced around the living room.

"Me? No. Totally not," I said.

"Sure," Mom replied, sarcasm oozing from her voice.

The knock on the door made me jump.

"Will you tell me what is wrong?" Mom asked.

"Nothing. Seems like everyone is here," I lied.

I hesitated at the door for a second before opening it. Two almost teenagers stood in front of me—Jane and John. One had freckles heavily covering her face, and the other had not a freckle in sight on his. Both had muted red coppery hair.

"Hey, Rai. I hear you're making ribs for us," they said in unison.

"Still doing that thing?" I cringed.

"What thing?" they asked, deadpan.

"Knock it off, you two," Ash's voice came from the side.

I froze. He came around the corner as the twins burst into laughter. He looked… tired. Like he hadn't slept in weeks, but there was something else, too.

"You look good," he said with a small smile.

"Uh… thanks," I managed to get out.

"Go help my parents with the casserole," Ash said and pushed the twins to the side. Then, turning to my mom, "Hey, Mrs. Eckles."

"Oh, Ash, have you been sleeping well? I have some herbal remedies for insomnia," Mom cooed.

"I'm fine, I promise," Ash said with his trademark little smirk.

"If you say so. I better go see how Marcus is doing with Lyra and Ulric."

Ash stepped out of the way to let my mom pass. As I went by him, he put his arm across the door. I moved back quickly and looked up at him, frightened. The look in his eyes wasn't what I expected. He looked... scared. That wasn't everything in those bright blue eyes, however. They were also filled with worry.

"Why won't you answer my calls?" he asked.

Chapter Eleven

"What do you mean? You haven't called. Also, why should I, after what you did? You can't just follow me back home and expect everything to be okay," I said, my voice steadier than I felt.

"Follow you? I've not left here since the twins started changing," Ash said, the confusion plain on his face.

"Don't try to lie to me. You chased away Tessa, Isiak, Corri, Keira, and every other vampire and human," I snapped, the anger threatening to come out.

"Tessa? She hasn't answered me either. What happened in Cali? I'm not lying, just ask my parents. I haven't left. Jane and John can already control their change, and they're constantly itching to fight. It's not just them… I feel off somehow that I can't explain."

I stared at him. He wasn't lying. I knew all of his tells, but I had seen him with my own eyes.

"I can't do this right now," I muttered. "Don't try to pull anything while my parents are around."

The look in his eyes almost made my anger falter. It was the same look I had seen in Tessa's eyes before she ran away. I slipped under his arm and headed for the yard where the food was being laid out.

"Hi, Mr. and Mrs. Ulfr," I greeted, forcing a smile.

"Rai! How have you been? How's that Tessa girl?" asked Ulric cheerfully.

Lyra elbowed him. His face fell as he realized the mistake.

"Tessa? Who is that?" asked Mom.

"Just… someone I met last year. It's no big deal," I mumbled as I hid my face.

"I expect a full explanation later," Mom said.

"Yes, Mom."

"Sorry," Ulric mouthed.

I just shrugged.

John and Jane tilted their heads at me. I couldn't tell if they were confused about my scent or if they wanted to see if they could get away with attacking me.

"So, when did Ash get back in town?" I asked as I set plates at a handmade wooden table we used for these family get-togethers.

"About a month," said Lyra. "I keep telling him he doesn't have to stay."

Ash shot a glance towards the twins, who were whispering to each other. "I'll go home when I'm sure everything is taken care of."

"Are you two having money issues?" asked Dad. "You know we would help. We could even do a bake sale."

"It's nothing serious," said Lyra. "Ash is just overreacting."

"Are you sure? I have seen Ash helping people out around town this whole month. I thought he was just being a thoughtful young man, but…" said Mom.

"Wait, you've seen him here all the time?" I asked a little

too quickly.

"Yes. He even helped me plant a new pear tree a couple of weeks before you got here."

"That was just last week, Mrs. Eckles," corrected Ash.

"Sure, if you want to conform to the government's form of time," Dad chimed in, though jokingly or seriously it was hard to tell.

I glanced at Ash as he laughed loudly. What the hell is going on? As soon as the twins had food in front of them, they tore into it like wild animals.

"Hey! Show some manners!" Ash scolded.

"No, it's fine. At least I know they like it," said Dad.

"It's not fine," Ash replied sternly. "Eat like you know what a spoon and fork are."

The twins looked up at him sheepishly and slowed down their feral feasting. He shook his head and went back to eating his own meal.

"This is really good," said Ulric. "There are two different ones?"

"Yep, me and Rai each made a batch," said Dad. "The ones on the right and the ones on the left are different."

"Hmm." Ulric grabbed one from each plate.

He chomped down on both at once. His face went into a thoughtful look as he chewed on one side of his mouth, then the other. My dad watched Ulric's face intently as he tried to decipher anything that would betray which he preferred.

"Can we go somewhere and talk?" Ash whispered over

the table as everyone paid attention to our fathers.

I looked down at my plate before replying, "Come back tonight like you used to."

His eyes glanced over at the twins. "I'll try…"

"Are they that bad?" I asked.

"They're constantly testing everything," sighed Ash.

"Marcus, I think this secret sauce of yours still is the best thing I ever tasted," Ulric said loudly after he swallowed.

"Hear that? I still got it," laughed my dad.

"Well, if you'd tell me what you put in it!" I said playfully.

"That ain't how this works. Gotta make your own instead of following those recipes you get on that fangled net," shot back Dad.

"Fine, fine. That's just one opinion. I'm sure the others think differently," I said.

"Nope, his," the twins chimed together.

"I didn't really taste the difference," Lyra said, though I could tell she was just trying to be nice.

I looked at Ash, who simply shrugged.

"Oh… fine. I know when I'm beat," I said with a melodramatic sigh.

Ash didn't stay long after dinner was over, but his parents did. I don't know what they talked about, but it was long after my parents' normal bedtime when they left. It was times like these that my parents broke out their homemade whiskey. I passed my time in my room, idly flipping through my phone as I waited to hear from Tessa or Ash. A random movie played on my TV, but I paid it no attention. I must have fallen asleep, because I woke up to the sound of tapping on my window. It took me a moment to realize where I was when I sat up. I had been in the middle of a dream that I couldn't remember. Thinking the taps had come from my dream, I went to lie back down when they came again.

I jumped up, remembering I told Ash to come, and opened my curtains. Ash stood there with a look that said, "Finally."

"Sorry," I whispered as I unlocked the window.

"I thought you weren't going to open it," he said as I climbed out.

Against my better judgment, I followed him to the tree line.

"So, what do you want?" I asked as he leaned against a tree.

"I want you to talk to me. What did I do? You've ignored me for weeks."

"I haven't ignored you. I left you back in Cali, and now you're here saying you never left."

"I'm telling you, I've not left this town since I got here last full moon. You know me. Do I look like I'm lying?"

"No… but I don't understand. You were acting weird. Tessa ran away after you hit her, because you two got into a fight when you made sure all the other vampires were gone," I insisted.

"If I wanted the vampires gone, why would I have made the werewolves come back here?" Ash asked, raising a brow.

"Look, I don't know, okay? I'm just telling you what happened. I came back here to figure out if something happened to you while you were here. Then Raulene and Lowell tell me that something has been creeping around their part of the woods. I didn't even know the Fairchilds were a werewolf family here."

Ash pushed off the tree. "Wait. What kind of something?"

"They didn't know."

"They didn't tell me something was near the border of our areas?"

"Lowell said even his dad had no idea."

"Okay, that will have to wait. First off… Do you know where Tessa is? Cause I would never hurt either of you. Second, even if all this happened, you didn't answer my calls or texts to tell me off?"

"I haven't gotten any calls or texts from you," I snapped.

He handed me his phone. There were pages of texts to me as I scrolled through. Also, multiple missed calls every day over the last week. In return, I showed him mine. There had been nothing from him. Same with Tessa since I had been back in town, no response. He tried to call me on speaker. I heard the ringing, but my phone did nothing. Next, I texted Casey: You okay? A few of seconds later came a reply: Yeah, I'm fine. I stared blankly at the screen. I tried to call Ash, but it went straight to voicemail. Then Tessa, the same thing.

"What the…" I whispered.

"Did anyone touch your phone?" asked Ash.

"Not that I know of. But… I have been followed by… something."

"And you're just now telling me this!" his voice a mixture of concern and anger.

"It's just a bird."

He gave me a skeptical look. "Explain."

"I met someone—a real scion. Around that time, a raven started following me. It's even followed me here."

"How did you find a scion? Never mind, we can talk about that later. How do you know it's the same bird?"

"Well, Mom pointed it out. One black eye, one silver. Not too many birds like that."

"Did you ever tell Tessa?"

"No. It was a bird, I wasn't too worried," I muttered.

"Birds can be omens… It might be trying to warn you. Whoever looked like me might be behind this."

"Maybe. I didn't think it was connected."

Just then, a loud caw pierced the air, and Ash tensed. The raven swooped down. As it flew away, a sharp pain lanced through my right ear. I clutched it as Ash stared into the sky. Fear was etched all over his face.

"What's its issue?" I groaned as I felt blood flowing down my hand.

"I… I don't know what that is. If that's the thing the Fairchilds are trying to track… This is bad," Ash mumbled.

He then looked at me, at my bloody hand, and paled. I took off my shirt to stem the blood flow.

"And it just got a lot worse," Ash whispered, his voice

trembling.

"Why?" I asked.

"It took a chunk of your earlobe. If it's what I think, it's a familiar."

"A what?"

Ash sighed. "I'll explain later. We need a phone, not one of ours, and we need it now."

"Well, you know how my parents just love to keep up with all the latest in technology. They have this nice new rotary phone and some fashionable cloth bandages for my ear," I said dryly.

"It'll have to work," Ash said and headed towards my parents' house.

As I followed, I texted Casey. 'I need a huge favor. I can't explain right now, but I'll try to when I can. Please go to the address I'm sending and tell me who is there. I know it's weird and I hate to ask you, but you're the only person I can.'

I sent the address. It was after midnight, so I didn't expect an answer right away. Part of me still wasn't convinced there was a second Ash. A moment later, I got back a question mark.

'I'm sorry, I can't explain further. I just need to put my mind at ease over something,' I replied.

When they didn't respond back, I just figured I had asked too much.

Chapter Twelve

As soon as we got back inside, Ash went straight to cleaning, then bandaging my ear.

"So, what's a familiar?" I asked, as he did.

Mostly to take my mind off the pain.

"It's old magic. It's a fae creature, disguised as an animal, bound to a practitioner of magic, and forced to do their bidding. From what I know, the summoner can even see through the creature's eyes," said Ash. "I've never seen one. I don't even know if it is one. All I do know is it's not a bird."

"Could whatever has summoned that creature also create zombies?" I asked.

"I don't know. Magic, or its usage, is not something I know about. Werewolves are around to just kill vampires," sighed Ash. "It's all we learn about. Anything else is just a guessing game when we face it. We both know the movies we've seen don't work in our favor."

"Well, you're an Alpha now," I said.

"So?"

"You can change things. We know most vampires are fine. You can turn your pack into something more."

"It's not that easy…"

"Nothing good ever is."

"I don't think I can make it as an Alpha. I couldn't even get a group to coexist with part of our family."

"We're young, we make mistakes, and you basically just became the leader. You'll find your way to make it seem easy as time goes by. Until then, you're going to need to ask for help. You have your dad or another Alpha who can give you some help. Whatever you can do, so that the next generation, like John and Jane, can know more and don't follow some archaic dogma. No offense."

He looked at me for a second, then laughed, "Dog... ma."

The laugh was a bit too loud as my dad burst out of his room, a baseball bat in hand. His eyes scanned the room in front of him until they landed on us. He lowered his bat and yawned.

"It's been too long since I've seen this," he said groggily and went back to his room.

"Sorry," Ash called out.

"Anyway," I said.

"You're right, as usual, but that's for a later time. We need to call Tessa."

He picked up the receiver and stared in confusion at the phone.

"I don't know how to work this," he said with a hand behind his head.

"Give that to me," I chuckled. "Always amazed me that the person who literally lived in the woods had better technology than my parents. Meanwhile, I was taught how to use all this archaic junk."

"Hey, you weren't exactly raised in town," Ash said with a smirk.

"Yeah, yeah, but at least I have a driveway," I joked as I dialed Tessa's number.

"Hello," Tessa answered, confusion in her voice.

"Oh, thank God you're okay," I said, letting out a sigh of relief.

"Rai? What number is this? What happened to your phone? Why haven't you answered anything I sent you? I have been so worried, I thought something had found a way to kill you," she cried into the phone.

"Did Keira find you?" I asked.

"Yes. She said you went home, but you've not answered me for days!"

"That's why I'm calling from my parents' house. Something is messing with us. Nothing that involves our phone goes through to the other person," I explained. "I also think a... familiar fae thing... is following me."

"What? Are you certain? Something that can control that is serious trouble."

"Can you tell me anything about them?" I asked.

"Rrruuuuunnnn," came a scratchy voice over the phone.

After that, the line was dead air. I cursed loudly.

"What?" asked Ash.

"Something cut the signal," I seethed.

He took the receiver from me, listened, set it in the cradle, checked it again, then slammed it down with a growl. His golden eyes oozed anger. That was the moment I believed in the two Ashes. The other Ash had never had his eyes change color. To solidify it, a new text came through. Casey had sent me a picture of Ash. He stood naked in the side yard, staring into the sky.

I looked up at Ash and then kissed him. As I pulled back, he stared at me, dumbfounded. I showed him the picture.

"What the hell?"

"A shapeshifter of some kind?" I asked.

"Tessa would have been able to smell the difference if it were. At least with the only shifters I know of. I have no idea what could do that to fool a vampire's senses," said Ash as he furrowed his brow.

By mid-morning, Ash sat next to me on a plane home. As soon as my mom woke up, we got her to drive us to the airport. I knew she wanted to ask why my ear was bandaged or why I was leaving so abruptly, but she said nothing except that she'd miss me and that I should visit again soon.

"What about the twins?" I asked as I held Ash's hand.

"I'll deal with them later if I need to. Right now, I need to make sure Tessa is safe. If I stay, I might hurt them when they do something out of pocket. I would feel even worse than I do now if I did that because of my rage. Coming with you, I can at least focus that rage on something that deserves to be ripped apart," Ash whispered, his eyes as gold as the dawn.

Casey was waiting for us as we got off the plane. Ash wrinkled his nose as he got close to Casey, but since Casey didn't seem to notice, I said nothing.

"I have the car like you wanted. Why did you need me?"

asked Casey.

"I needed to use your phone," I said. "Casey, this is Ash. Ash, Casey."

"Wasn't he the person I sent you a picture of?" asked Casey.

"You look familiar," said Ash.

"I promise I will explain later," I said as we got into the car. "Can I use your phone?"

"So you keep saying," muttered Casey.

He handed me his phone, and I called Tessa as I drove out of the parking garage.

"Tessa, listen, I don't know how much time we have. Tell me where you are," I said quickly when she answered.

She gave me the address, and as she said she loved me, the line went dead.

"Caaaan't hiiiide," the scratchy voice rasped again.

I handed the phone back to Casey and sighed.

"Okay, so, some creature is out to keep me separated from my husband," I said as I pointed to Ash, "and my wife. I don't want you to be involved in this, but I needed your help. There's a lot going on that I don't understand, and I don't know what will happen when this is over. If I'm still alive, I promise I will sit down with you and go over everything."

"Like how the guy I took a picture of stepped off a plane with you?" Casey asked.

"Exactly. I don't want you wrapped up in this any more than you already are, so I'm going to drop you off at your dorm."

"Fine."

Ash just eyed me as I drove. The dorms were out of the way, and even though I was extremely anxious to get to Tessa, getting Casey as far away from the drama about to unfold was also important to me. I truly wanted to keep them as safe as I could. They didn't deserve to be part of whatever hell was happening with my life at the moment. The evening traffic brought out my road rage as we inched down the highway. It reminded me why I never drive in this town.

After what felt like hours, I got Casey home and sped away to Tessa. She had found an abandoned JCPenney store to use as a place to stay.

"Tessa!" I called out.

Before the words even stopped echoing, I was pinned against the wall. Her hands held me by the wrists above my head, and her lips were pressed against mine. Her tongue found its way to mine, and I let out a little moan. It was minutes before she pulled away.

"Oh, how I've missed you," she said, a smile spread across her bright red lips.

The smile faded as quickly as it formed, replaced by a scowl, and she turned to face Ash. She stood in front of me protectively. Ash's blue eyes were filled with tears that streamed down his cheeks.

"What's he doing here?" Tessa asked coldly.

"Tessa... My love... My heart," Ash said softly, "That wasn't me. I'm so sorry that I wasn't there for you."

Her body language told me that she didn't believe him. I saw her tense as she was getting ready to strike. I stepped behind her and wrapped my arms around her waist.

"He's not lying," I whispered in her ear. "Whoever… or whatever… was in our house, it was not Ash."

"I don't know how you tricked Rai, but I know it was you. I know you as well as you know yourself. Your smell is unmistakable, it's seared into my being," growled Tessa.

"Exactly. You know me. You've been inside my head, you've felt everything I have. Can you believe I would do any of those things Rai told me about?"

I felt her body tense up in my arms. I held her tighter.

"I can prove it," I said.

She glanced back at me, uncertainty flickering in her eyes.

"Think about his eyes. Every time he's angry, his wolf eyes come out. Not once did that happen with that thing in our house."

"That proves nothing," she muttered, but the doubt in her was clear.

"Our parents also told me he'd been in our hometown this whole time," I continued, releasing her and pulling out my phone. "Then, while I talked to you this morning—while I was with Ash—I received this."

I showed her the picture that Casey had taken.

"I… it's… how?" stuttered Tessa as she stared at the screen.

"I don't know. I aim to find out who did this," Ash said as he moved closer. "Whoever did this to my heart and to my soul will be ripped to shreds if it's the last thing I do."

His golden eyes shimmered in the water, still falling from his eyes.

"Who was that… we…" shuddered Tessa.

"Shh," whispered Ash as she wrapped his arms around both of us. "Don't think about them."

Tessa broke down, burying her face in his chest. Ash gently ran his fingers through her hair. I stepped back. No matter what came next, I knew everything I needed was in front of me.

Chapter Thirteen

"Where are Isiak and Corri?" Ash asked after a moment.

"Why?" I asked.

"They're old. They might know what we're facing," explained Ash.

"I'm not sure. There are places we can check for them. But before we do that, what happened to your ear and nose?" asked Tessa.

"I got punched in the face by a new friend, on accident, for the nose," I muttered. "As for the ear... the familiar took a chunk out of it."

Tessa furrowed her brow. "Let's put the new friend thing on the back burner. A piece of you being taken is not good. Like at all. Who knows what a mage can do with a piece of a god—or even just the blood of a god."

Ash shrugged. "Their new friend is... interesting."

"If it's who I think it is, the one that created the familiar, they'll only think I'm half god at least," I shrugged.

"Who do you think it is?" asked Tessa.

"Whoever did the magic for Cazimir to create the zombies."

Tessa tilted her head, thinking. "Hmm... it could be possible. They'd definitely have the skill for summoning a familiar if they could reanimate corpses."

"Let's go find Isiak and Corri first. We can worry about that later," said Ash.

"There's a beach house that we can start at," said Tessa.

As soon as the sun was down, we were off to the beach in the rental car. Tessa directed me to a tiny bungalow not far from where Ash usually did his surfing.

"They aren't here," Ash said as we pulled up.

"How do you know?" I asked, confused.

"No st—smell of vampires. Nobody has been here in a while," he explained.

"Well, let's just go next," I said.

After going to half a dozen more places, I was convinced that we weren't going to find them.

"Maybe they left town. You said they moved around a lot anyway," I said as we sat in front of the latest empty house.

"Not a shot. They'd be somewhere near, plotting their revenge. They were chased out of their house by someone they had agreed with at first," said Tessa. "There is one more place we can go, but I didn't think they would know about it."

"What? Where?" I asked.

"I set up a safehouse when Ash—fake Ash—started chasing the other vampires away. I didn't want them to go to the dark side, so I just moved them and the staff to a second house. It's where Keira is at right now."

Pretty soon, we were there. I had expected a nice house, not unlike where we lived. What I got was an old, boarded apartment complex that I had heard was meant to be demolished ages ago. It was five stories tall, and I don't know how many rooms it had.

"Hello, Tessa, my dear," came Isiak's sing-song voice. "Explain why you brought that thing with you."

"It's unbelievable, but that thing at our house is not Ash. Something is impersonating him," said Tessa firmly.

"Impossible," scoffed Isiak. "Skinwalkers, changelings, nor trickster gods can make their scent an exact copy of what they shift into."

"What about with magic?" I asked.

"N…" started Corri.

Isiak shut her down with a look, then put a finger to his chin in thought.

"Well?" Ash pressed.

"Nothing I have ever witnessed, and I have witnessed more than you could ever fathom, could do something like that," Isiak said slowly.

"So, it's not possible," I muttered, dejected.

"I didn't say that, child. I said I haven't witnessed it. However, I have heard rumors. Grigori, before his untimely assassination from those Romanovs, swore he was on the verge of creating something you would call a clone of Nikolai. Some even say that he had succeeded, and that is what led to his death, along with the fall of the Romanov dynasty," mused Isiak. "If someone had the research, and a will as strong as Rasputin's… maybe. But I don't believe the tales of mortal men. The sheer amount of power needed to create life? It would destroy them. It's black magic at its finest. I've seen people combust just trying to do basic reanimation."

"What about a mage someone like Cazimir would use? He wouldn't use a normal human. He'd find someone special, right?" asked Ash.

"Assuming the dark magic that made him didn't also let him use magic, then it could be possible," admitted Isiak. "But we can't know what skills he possessed."

Ash frowned. "So, basically, if what you say is true, then I was cloned. Wouldn't that make the clone have the same memories and personality as me?"

Isiak pinched the bridge of his nose. "It's magic, dog. Not one of your crude little science fiction movies."

"Wait, so you're telling me I'm not Beetlejuice?" asked Ash, deadpan.

The vampires stared blankly at him while I burst out laughing. Ash started laughing too, pleased with himself.

"What's so funny?" asked Tessa, confused.

"It's a really old movie," I choked through my laughter.

"No, I know what Beetlejuice is, but he doesn't clone himself."

"I'll show you what the joke is later," I giggled. "Now's not the time for movie trivia."

Ash grinned at me while Tessa rolled her eyes.

"So, will I die if it dies?" Ash asked, voice suddenly serious again.

"How should I know? Though I do imagine Grigori would have wanted Nikolai dead when he was replaced," shrugged Isiak.

"Let's not take that chance. We'll just capture the fake

99

Ash and then question it," I said.

It hadn't even occurred to me that they could be linked in some way like that until Ash brought it up.

"You two need to sleep first," said Tessa.

"But…" I began.

"No. I want to end this as fast as you do, but it can wait until tomorrow night," Tessa said sternly. "Ash looks like he hasn't slept in days, and you're over here laughing at a joke nobody understands."

"Fine," Ash and I finally said.

She was right. I hadn't slept in over twenty-four hours, and Ash… well, he had circles under his eyes during dinner last night. We were shown an apartment we could use. As we lay down, I didn't expect to sleep right away. I crawled on top of him as I kissed his neck. The mood fizzled fast as I heard a loud snore. Ash had fallen asleep almost as soon as his head hit the pillow. I rolled off of him and found sleep easier than I thought, falling nearly instantly. I woke up as Tessa crawled into bed with us. It was about dawn, so I wasn't ready to get up. She curled up against me with her head resting on my shoulder, and I drifted back to sleep.

The next time I woke up, Tessa was already awake. Ash was drooling, still asleep. She paced around the room wearing the same clothes she had been wearing the night before. Her ears twitched, and she looked over at me.

"You're awake. You two must have needed sleep," she said.

"How did you know I woke up?" I asked.

"Your breathing changed," she shrugged.

"Of course."

I motioned for her to come to me, and she climbed into the bed next to me.

"Go brush your teeth first," she said as I leaned in to kiss her.

I rolled my eyes and groaned. "I don't have a toothbrush. I didn't pack to be here."

"Guess no kisses for you," she said.

I stuck my tongue out at her, and she smiled at me. Ash sat up and rubbed his eyes.

"Is it time to go yet?" he yawned.

"We should make some kinda plan first," I said.

"No plan. Too tired. Let's just go," mumbled Ash.

"We're just going to try to capture a werewolf. Should be easy," Tessa said sarcastically.

"Sure… But I'm better. Probably can't even change without the full moon," Ash muttered.

"Let's go then," I said.

It didn't take long for us to be at the gate to the community where the house was. We parked the car outside the gate and went in on foot.

"Rai… you should stay in the car," Ash said.

"He's right," agreed Tessa.

"Why?" I asked.

"Because you're not going to be able to fight a werewolf without killing it," replied Ash.

"I know you can revive, but seeing you die… that's

rough," added Tessa, her voice quieter.

"I am not going to let you two go in there alone. What happens if the other Ash comes out? It would take too long for me to know if it was the real one or not. Then they might kill me while I try to figure it out," I argued.

They stared at me.

"No. I am not being left behind just because I'm not supernatural," I said firmly.

"Well, actually…" began Tessa.

"You're probably the most supernatural out of us all," Ash finished for her.

"You know what I meant."

"You're just gonna follow us, aren't you?" asked Tessa.

"You know it," I confirmed.

They both sighed, but started walking without saying another word. I followed behind them, wondering what I could do to help them. As we got to the house, every light was on, a jarring sight compared to how it usually looked.

"If this is the norm, the light bill is going to be astronomical," joked Ash.

"Not now," snapped Tessa.

"Look, I'm nervous. I need to do it," murmured Ash.

"He's not even in the house," said Tessa after a moment. "I guess that's why your friend was able to get the photo. He's out back."

"That will never not be weird," I muttered as I followed them around the house.

We moved slowly and quietly, which for them was easy,

but I felt like I was making a racket. They didn't turn around to say anything, though, so maybe I was just being paranoid. As we looked around the corner of the house into the backyard, there he was. He stood there looking up at the sky, naked. His head turned at an unnatural angle and locked eyes with mine.

"Welcome back," purred fake Ash as he licked his lips.

Chapter Fourteen

Seeing both Ashes at the same time was jarring.

"I've looked everywhere for you, Rai," said fake Ash. "I wasn't meant to scare you off. You just had to come back at the wrong time."

The way it said my name, the same mispronounced way Ash said it, made my blood run cold.

"You thought this creepy thing was me?" shuddered Ash.

It lurched towards us, its bones cracked as it did.

"It obviously didn't move or seem this weird," said Tessa.

I don't know what compelled me, but as I watched the way the body moved, I couldn't help but walk forward. I heard Ash and Tessa yelling my name too late. When it registered to me that they were saying anything, I was almost touching fake Ash. It loomed over me with a twisted smile on its face.

"We have what we need now. The blood of a godling," said fake Ash.

"You've got nothing," I croaked out.

I looked back at the yelling Ash and Tessa. They struggled against something that I couldn't see.

"Let them go," I demanded as my senses came back to me.

"Sure," said fake Ash in a way I knew meant he was going to kill them.

Without thinking, my fist shot out and struck it in the jaw. I howled in pain as my bones shattered. It was like I hit a brick wall full force.

"That was… unexpected," it said.

Then a large arm went straight through my chest. Fake Ash had gone through me all the way to his bicep. The familiar fire spread through my body as I gasped for air. My lungs were destroyed. Suffocation was a new one for me. I don't recommend trying it. The last thing I remembered before the fire consumed my body was falling to the ground with the arm still inside me. When I woke up, it was uncomfortable. I was lying on something that was large and hard. As I shifted to get it out from under me, I realized it was a severed arm. The same arm that had been impaled in me. I quickly looked around me and saw bits and pieces of Ash scattered around. I immediately panicked. Tessa had to be fighting the creature, otherwise she would be near me. She always was when I died.

When I finally saw her, it was not how I had expected it to be. Ash and she were bathed in the blood of the creature, which was the most normal part of what I saw. Both were naked. Ash lay in the grass on his back, and Tessa knelt next to him. As I stood up, Tessa looked over at me from where she knelt. Her purple eyes were bright as she licked the blood off of Ash's lower head. He moaned softly.

"Guys?" I asked.

I wasn't sure if I was turned on or weirded out.

"The blood… it's so intoxicating," Tessa purred.

As her mouth wrapped around Ash's member, I rushed to find the hose. I didn't know what was going on, but the blood had to be doing something to them. Ash's grunts of pleasure caused me to fumble as I unwrapped the hose. I rushed to turn on the water, then hurried back to them. When I returned, Tessa was face down in the grass, her back arched, with Ash behind her in his hybrid form.

"Harder!" screamed Tessa in ecstasy.

I felt myself growing hot as I stood rooted in place. I wanted to join in. I tilted my head and watched Ash thrust into her. His low guttural grunts mixed with her loud moans caused something primal to stir inside me. The hose nearly slipped from my hands. Then I saw something that brought me back to the reality of the situation. Between each of his thrusts, his claws raked across her back, tearing flesh and spraying blood. Even worse, it was the clawing that made her scream harder. I turned the nozzle to high pressure and blasted Ash in the face. He fell back, mostly in surprise, and out of Tessa. I then turned the hose to Tessa as she looked up at me with disappointment.

"I think you two need to cool off," I said as the blood washed away from her.

When Ash stood up, he was back in human form, and I blasted him with the hose. Soon they stood there, naked, soaked, and confused.

"What happened to my back?" groaned Tessa.

"Why do I feel like I need to take a bath in lava?" asked Ash.

"The blood of that thing had some magic in it. It made you sex craved. I think it also made you want to be tortured.

Mostly it was hot," I said as I stared at their naked bodies. "Come with me."

They followed willingly as I took each of them by the hand. I led them inside with thoughts of taking them to our bedroom. But I couldn't wait that long. My body wanted them in ways I hadn't ever felt before. Maybe it was because of what I had just seen, maybe the rebirth had done something to me, or maybe it was because I hadn't been with either of them in so long. Whatever the reason, the bedroom was too far away. I pushed them both against the wall and got down on my knees. I took Ash in my mouth as my hand went between Tessa's legs.

"Rai…" moaned Ash. "You… aaaah… have blood… aaahh… on your… back."

I stopped in the middle of sucking and pulled away. Well, that explained everything. That stupid arm. I cursed loudly and stood up. I was suddenly aware that I stood in the hallway naked. It hadn't even occurred to me after the rebirth that my clothes were destroyed… like always. I turned away and went to the closest shower and started to scrub myself with the hottest water I could stand. When I finally got out, Ash and Tessa were also dressed and freshly showered.

"I thought magic didn't work on me. Yet I was compelled to walk to that thing… and then with what just happened," I said.

"It wasn't magic. At least not purely magic. Whatever was making me get off on the pain in my back was magic that tampered with my brain. But the sex… that was pure pheromones," explained Tessa. "And I think the way that thing moved was some sort of hypnotism, which is also not magic. Normal humans do it all the time to make people forget things like when they cluck like chickens."

"Can that actually happen?" I asked, astonished.

"Why yes, darling. Just a bit of science and pattern movements. Very rarely is it mixed with magic," came Isiak's voice. "Whoever did this is someone I wish to meet."

"Well, if you follow that thing to its master, you might get your wish," I said as I pointed at a raven that watched us from the window.

"Is that what you called a familiar?" asked Tessa, with a hint of fear in her voice.

It flew away as I moved toward it.

"Yes. Why?" I asked.

"Hmm," was all Isiak offered.

"What?" Ash and I asked in unison.

"That wasn't a fae," whispered Tessa.

"The dog, it seems, is woefully inept when it comes to the other creatures of our world," sighed Isiak, pinching the bridge of his nose.

"What is it?" I asked.

"A skinwalker of sorts. Not one in the truest sense of the word, but one, nonetheless. That is probably the mage you are looking for. To think it has the power to change its own form to something as small as a raven," said Isiak, his voice full of intrigue.

"Least I knew it wasn't a real skinwalker," huffed Ash.

"Yes, yes. I'm so proud of you," Isiak said dismissively.

"Can any of you track it?" I asked hopefully.

"How? There is no trail. We cannot fly," replied Isiak.

I took a deep breath to push down the rising anger. Once again, we had nothing to go on.

"There has to be something we can do. Do they have a den? A coven that is easy to stand out? Do they like caves?" I asked.

"Oh, child, a mage is basically just a human. They will have the stench of magic to them that a normal human doesn't, but they can be anywhere. There are several that live in this very city. However, none of them have the power that is needed for this," explained Isiak. "Dark magic changes the essence of whoever uses it, but it does not change the outside. That makes it hard to tell who the user is without seeing it firsthand."

I sat down, feeling inept but frustrated.

"We will just have to scour the city," sighed Ash.

"If they are even in the city," chimed in Corri quietly.

"What about Rai's new friend? When exactly did you meet them?" asked Ash suddenly. "They definitely had a strange scent about them."

"They're not part of this," I replied. "They're also a scion, so they can't be a mage."

"That's untrue," Isiak cut in. "However, was this the same one I saw you with?"

Tessa frowned. "Has everyone met this person but me?"

"Yes, to both of those things," I said.

"Oh, that was no scion," laughed Isiak in amusement.

"I knew it!" exclaimed Ash.

I stared at them skeptically. "What are they then?"

"They are nothing I've ever seen," answered Ash.

"Shocking," said Isiak dryly. "What it is does not matter. If the mage was controlling it, I think it would have broken down like that simulacrum you took out."

"It never hurts to go and make sure," said Corri.

"No! Casey has nothing to do with this," I said as I got to my feet.

"I still think it's a large coincidence that you made a friend that isn't quite human just as a thing that shapeshifts comes after us," said Ash.

I knew from his voice it was that same jealousy he had when I met Tessa, but what he said made me start to doubt myself. Casey said they didn't know how to control their changing, but what if it was a lie? Did they actually do it unconsciously based on how they felt?

"Look… they've been extremely understanding about a lot of things. I'm not going to let you interrogate them and then have to explain that I didn't trust them. There are some things that cannot be faked," I said. "The loneliness in their voice and eyes when we met—that was real."

"Which makes…" started Ash.

"No," said Tessa firmly. "I trust Rai's instincts. That same thing is what made us friends… and more."

She stood next to me and laid her head on my shoulder. I wrapped an arm around her and smiled. It was easy to tell she didn't trust the person she had never met, but that she trusted me made things better.

"We will get some rest for the night. Tomorrow, we find this mage," said Tessa.

"Okay," replied Ash.

Something unspoken was said between Tessa and Isiak. I had no idea what, but Isiak just nodded and left with Corri.

"Where are they going?" I asked.

"Searching. What's the point of a whole vampire clan at your disposal if you don't use it?" asked Tessa.

"What if they find something?"

"Then they come and get me."

As the minutes turned to hours, Ash and I decided to show Tessa why we had laughed at the Beetlejuice joke. It was an ancient movie called Multiplicity. Michael Keaton cloned himself to try and be a better husband, while also still being a terrible husband, while getting jealous of himself, and sort of learning to be a better husband. She left halfway through the movie, unamused by the very outdatedness of it, to go watch some slasher movie. I fell asleep with my head on Ash's lap as we continued to watch it.

Chapter Fifteen

My dream started off pleasantly. The three of us were on a blue and white checkered blanket amongst a field of sunflowers. The sun felt refreshing as it blazed overhead. My skin seemed to radiate as I lay there. Ash fed Tessa grapes as she fanned herself with a silk folding fan. Everything was perfect. I started to get brighter as the world around me grew darker. I seemed to be absorbing even the light of the sun until it was just me as the sole light source. As I looked around the place where Ash and Tessa had been, there were just two piles of ash, and the blanket was no longer there. The field around me that had once been filled with luscious grass and sunflowers was just a wasteland.

"Everything that exists turns to ash in the end. Why should you care about things that will end while you continue to exist and grow, Phoenix?" asked a calm, old voice.

The sun burst into existence again, though my brightness didn't diminish at all. I somehow knew it was the sun that talked to me.

"Aren't you going to die in an ever-expanding explosion?" I asked. "Yet we still need you."

"This avatar will do this as so many of my other ones have and others are in the process of doing," said the sun. "Maybe my true form will die when Apophis is awakened and allowed to escape, while I'm left to reach out from my slumber as avatars. My son's son's son could very well be the one to end me. I cannot see my fate as I sleep."

"Okay… time to wake up. I need to lay off whatever it is I ate before I fell asleep," I muttered.

"You have not answered my question."

"What question? Why do I care about Ash and Tessa? Because during those days I felt alone, when I was at my most hopeless, when I felt invisible to the entire world, they were there," I confessed. "When I'm not sure I have a reason to be alive, they give me one. It's what we as people do for each other."

"There lies the contradiction. You are not these things you call people. You have killed the only remaining beings on that world that could ever hope to touch your lifespan, Phoenix. The fake bat will try to live alongside you, but its lifespan is as insignificant to you as the fake wolf's lifespan will be to it," declared the sun. "Cast them aside and become what you truly are."

"Even if I did believe you, I would never do that. I would raze the planet if anything happened to them. I would hunt down anyone who hurts them or tries to keep me away from them," I stated.

"So be it. Osiris was never this way. Though it remains to be seen if you are still better than Set."

The light faded away, and I found myself standing in the middle of a strange house. A woman muttered curses as she hunched over a cage. Inside it sat a very aged Tinkerbell.

"I'll have to catch a new one," croaked the crone.

A black feather sat on an open windowsill. Moments later, I was dragged out of the house to see it sitting in a cove that overlooked the ocean. Then I was rapidly dragged to the closest road, then down streets I half-recognized, until I stood over my body, lying asleep. I tumbled into it as if I had been shoved. I shot up, feeling as though I had been falling, and my sudden movements startled Ash awake.

"What's wrong?" he gasped as he looked around.

"Nothing," I yawned. "Just a dream."

I remembered everything so clearly, unlike most of my dreams. As I sat up, I noticed it was daytime already.

"Does Tinkerbell exist?" I asked.

"Huh?" asked Ash.

"You know… tiny fairy things that glow."

"I would guess so. Everything else humans use in stories are real," shrugged Ash. "Why?"

"It was just my dream."

I explained what my dream had been. I almost expected him to laugh, but he just looked thoughtfully at me.

"Dreams can be prophetic. Do you know how to get to this house?" asked Ash.

"Yes. If it's real anyway."

"We need to wait for Tessa, but then we should go check."

"Do you think we'll find anything?" I asked.

He nodded. It was his confidence that made me believe it, too. As I went up to go get something to drink, my phone rang. It was a call from Casey.

"Hey," I answered. "Sorry, I've been M.I.A. I haven't forgotten that I need to explain so many things."

"That's not why I called," Casey said with fear in her

voice. "I think someone was in my room last night."

"Did your roommate come back early?" I asked, concerned. "Did you call campus security? Or even the police?"

"No, she would never come back before she had to. What if it was that thing that followed me that one night? What would security or police be able to do to something like that? We don't even know what that is," she said. "I know you said not to worry… but I can't help but to. I don't understand any of this or why they would want to hurt me."

"Is anything missing or moved?" I asked as calmly as I could. "Maybe someone is just playing a trick on you."

My mind raced with the worst fears and Isiak's words. Casey wasn't immune to the supernatural. What if the thing that followed them was an enemy of whatever they were? Did other creatures have the werewolf and vampire rivalry?

"Nothing looks out of place. My window was open when I woke up, though. I also found a black feather next to my closet door," she said.

"Have you opened it?" I asked.

"No. Should I?"

I heard the sound of a door creaking.

"No!" I yelled. "Get out of there now!"

There was a scream, followed by a loud cackle, before the line went dead.

"Are you okay?" Ash asked as he came into the kitchen.

I didn't answer him as I dropped my phone. I ran as fast as I could out of the house and towards the dorms. Ash jogged beside me. He didn't say anything as he kept pace with me. I hated that I didn't have his speed at times like this. When I got to Casey's room, their door was open and there were a few feathers scattered around.

"What happened? Who lives here?" Ash asked.

"Casey," I said, out of breath.

I collapsed onto the floor to catch my breath.

"That mage's scent is all over the room," Ash said with his nose wrinkled.

"How did they get taken in the middle of the day?" I asked as I slammed my fist on the floor.

"Maybe it's a trap. That's the only thing that it could be," Ash said.

"I don't care if it is, I have to go get Casey."

"We will. If the house you saw is real, we will be there tonight. We'll need help," Ash said as he knelt down next to me.

"What if something bad happens while I wait?" I cried.

"I understand what you're going through, but we can't just walk into that mage's lair."

"I can," I said and stood up.

Ash grabbed me by the shoulder. I turned to glare at him.

"I don't know what a mage can do. I know scions are meant to be immune to magic… but don't forget, you're not a scion. That creature also has a piece of your ear."

The concern in his voice took the wind from my sails. I leaned against him and sobbed. I felt worthless as I stood

116

in my friend's room. He rubbed my back and said nothing. When I had no tears left to cry, we walked back to our house. I think I fell asleep again, but it wasn't restful at all. A small, gentle hand woke me up. My bloodshot eyes looked up at Tessa as she stood over me.

"Are you okay?" she asked.

Ash had apparently told her what had happened. I sat up and shook my head.

"Let's go," Tessa said as she held her hand out.

I took her hand and stood up. I led them through the streets that my dream had taken me until we were at the cove I had seen.

"If it's here… It's in there," I said somberly.

I was surrounded not just by the normal four of Ash, Tessa, Isiak, and Corri, but a half dozen other vampires I had not learned the names of. What was even more surprising was that Greg, along with a few other werewolves from the surf team, had come too.

"Well, hopefully this will not be too much of an overkill," said Isiak as he looked around.

"I don't know what we're going to walk into," said Tessa.

"I still think this is a trap," said Ash. "So I want to be prepared."

I stepped forward, and everyone went in front of me.

"I'm the one who can't die," I growled. "I'm going in first."

I stormed past them and stomped towards the entrance.

117

Isiak laughed in amusement and was the first to follow me. Which didn't bother me that much. If something were going to kill me, I wouldn't exactly be sad if he were there to also take it. I was only half-shocked that the house was actually there.

"Hmm, guess this dream of yours was a prophecy," Isiak scoffed.

"Sure. The sun is definitely known for being prophetic," I mumbled as I stood outside the door.

The door opened inward as we stood there, and the rest came up behind us.

"Do come in, you three," said the crone.

Even though there were a handful of us, I knew who she meant. Apparently, so did Ash and Tessa. After I went in, Tessa tested the boundary of the house and found she was able to walk through. Isiak tried to go in after her but was unable to put his foot inside the threshold. The weirdest part was, after Ash came in, Greg tried to go in and also couldn't.

"Looks like we're barred... somehow," mused Greg.

"Well, I appreciate you all coming anyway," Ash said right before the door slammed closed.

A fire burned in the center of the adjacent room. The crone sat on the far side of it. The fairy I had seen had been discarded in the corner, dead. Or so I assumed.

"Rai!" Casey shouted as I stepped into the room.

She was in a large cage suspended off the floor.

"Casey!" I started to move towards her.

I saw Ash and Tessa frozen in mid-step, and I stopped.

118

"Demigods are hard ones to break. But if you get a piece of them and use some esoteric magic, even they can be brought down," croaked the crone.

I didn't pay attention to what she was saying as I looked at Casey. She looked different. Older. I think there was even gray in her hair.

"Are you okay?" I asked.

She shook her head.

"I am talking to you!" snapped the crone.

"What are you doing to my friend?" I turned towards the crone.

"Using it to fuel my power. Why use my own life force when I can use the life force of others?"

"It hurts," Casey said as she doubled over.

Her form seemed to be unstable. It flickered back and forth between genders as they convulsed on the floor of the cage. The crone's laugh caused me to shift my gaze back to her. Something in her hand glowed brightly.

"So, I have caught the thing that somehow killed Cazimir," said the crone. "I wish I knew how you did that. But he will rise again with the help of your two friends over there. Maybe he will be even stronger if I use the body of a scion."

I looked back at Ash and Tessa. I couldn't afford to do what I did to Cazimir because they were here. But I didn't know what else I could do to help them. Their faces were frozen in grimaces of pain. While I could tell from their eyes that they were conscious, I didn't know what was going on with them.

Chapter Sixteen

"What are you doing to my friends?" I asked through gritted teeth.

"Just keeping them frozen as I drain their energy. It seems like my trick to keep you quiet and frozen is not working perfectly," said the crone.

I took a step forward and smiled. The look on her face was priceless, a slack-jawed look as she looked down at her hand.

"Let all three of them go. None of them had anything to do with killing Cazimir. It was all me," I said angrily. "And if you continue to hurt them, I will do the same to you."

The corner of her mouth twitched, then went into a smile. I didn't see what hit me as I flew through the wall of the house and into the wall of the cove.

"Are you done toying with them?" asked a gruff voice from inside the house. "Can I kill them now?"

I stood up, and the world began to spin. As blood dripped into my starry vision, I stumbled towards the Rai-shaped hole in the wall. I blinked away the stars in my eyes and wiped away the blood to see a huge wolfman with pure black fur. It carried Ash in one arm and Tessa in the other.

"Drop them!" I said as loudly as I could.

It was barely a whimper, but the werewolves' ears perked up and they looked at me.

"It's up. Can I eat it?" asked the werewolf.

"Luca, as long as I hold this fragment of him, then yes. His blood is just that of a mortal while this spell lasts," explained the crone.

Luca dropped my friends and stalked towards me. I couldn't react as one paw wrapped around my torso and lifted me until I was face to face with the big snout. I had flashbacks to Cazimir and Yujin as I stared into the nostrils of the thing that held me.

"Hmm, you don't smell any different," said Luca.

He looked back at the crone.

"The spell works," the crone assured him.

He looked at me with a look of uncertainty in his eyes. His tongue whipped out and licked the blood off my face. After a moment, a grin spread across his face. I grew worried that perhaps some of that magic had taken hold. Luca opened his mouth wide, then closed it. A grimace spread across his features. He dropped me and I fell limply to the ground as he yelped in pain.

"Idiot," I said in a pained laugh.

Fire spread across Luca's body starting from his chest. White, hot, and so intense I had to crawl back as I closed my eyes. There was one final howl and then silence. The fire was gone, and I was covered in the ashes of Luca.

"How?" exclaimed the crone.

"Whatever you believed was mostly a lie," I said as I lay there. "Now, can I just get my friends and go. I'm tired of people dying around me. Also tired of being in pain."

"You have not experienced pain yet. I will show you true pain," the crone said as she stood over me.

"Give me a minute. I'll get right to you. Then we can have a nice little talk over some tea," I mumbled.

"First, I will kill your friends. Using the life force of an alpha werewolf and a vampire tethered to him could fuel any spell I want. Then, I kill you and figure out why my magic is struggling with you."

I sat up and glared at her. "Old lady, I don't know what you think you're going to accomplish, but it isn't going to be much if you touch a hair on my friends. Those three are off limits."

She patted me on the head. "Children should never know better than to speak to their betters."

She grabbed me by the hair and pulled me to my feet as I yelped. She dragged me to where she had been when I first came in and threw me to the ground.

"You are constantly trouble. What about you is so special?" wondered the crone.

"I'd tell you, but I think having some secrets is what's keeping me alive," I croaked.

"You're smarter than most I have at my feet. I have ways to get you to talk, however."

Ash yelled in pain. I looked at him and saw blood running from his mouth.

"I can make it where his insides turn to nothing. All while using the life of the other," said the crone.

Tessa seemed to shrivel as the crone talked.

"If you let them go, I'll tell you everything. I'll tell you how Cazimir died too," I pleaded.

"Oh, I think I know that already. However, I do wonder more about how you survived. I have never seen a werewolf turned to ash."

"Whatever you want. Just let them go. I'll even let you use me to fuel your magic," I said as I got to my knees.

"Hmm, that is very tempting. The things I could do using all of you," laughed the crone.

"So, is it a deal?" I asked.

"Why don't I just trap you here and use all four of you?" the crone asked.

"I refuse," I said as I struggled to my feet. "You let my friends go and live, or I'm burning this whole thing to the ground."

"You wouldn't risk hurting your friends. And a fire is nothing to my power, I would just use your friend's life to get rid of it."

I felt my body growing hotter, a familiar feeling but different than the usual burning when I died. The crone stepped back with a sharp gasp. I looked at my arms, and it was glowing as bright as the sun. The crone yelped as whatever was in her hand flared with a light that couldn't be contained by her grip. She opened her hand, and ashes fell to the ground.

"Who are you? What are you doing?" she screeched.

"Putting an end to all of this," I said, my voice reverberated around me. "I am more than you and your pathetic kind could hope to fathom."

Heat radiated off my body, and the crone stepped back as a heat mirage appeared around me. I looked down at my body as it moved of its own accord.

"This is impossible. What are you?"

"The end. At least for you," came my voice, but it wasn't me speaking.

I stepped forward, and my shoes melted away as I did. The laugh of the crone made me falter. The screams of my friends brought me back to my body, and I fell to the ground as my body felt like lead.

"You care about these people. As long as I have them, I am safe. It doesn't matter what you are, you can't risk them," laughed the crone.

I tried to feel the fire inside again, but there was nothing there. I sighed as I lay there. I couldn't move; my body felt so heavy after doing whatever I had. The effort to move my head to see my friends was all I could manage. Tessa looked like a skeleton, Casey's body was arched in almost a perfect U-shape, their mouth opened unnaturally wide, and Ash sagged against an unseen barrier. His eyes were closed, but I could just barely make out his chest moving to let me know he was alive. The crone circled me as she chanted something in a language I couldn't begin to comprehend. It took me a bit to realize she was also drawing symbols around me as she did.

"This isn't going to work," I managed to get out.

Even my mouth seemed heavy as I talked. She didn't stop chanting as she circled me a second time. While she did whatever she had in mind, my body started to feel normal and my head stopped spinning, but I stayed where I was. Only one thought came into my head: hit this old woman in the face when she was off guard. Eventually, she stopped and looked down at her handiwork with a smug look.

"Now let's see you escape that," the crone said with a slight chuckle.

I stood up and glared at her.

"Rai just run," croaked out Casey.

"Get away," muttered Ash.

"You can't win," breathed Tessa.

The words swirled around me, coming from every direction.

"You're not good enough," said Ash.

"This is too much for you," said Tessa.

"You promised to help me," said Casey.

A vortex swirled around me, and the laughing of the crone mixed in with the cries of my friends.

"Stop it!" I cried out and fell to my knees.

"You are useless. Why did you even come?" asked Ash.

Tessa said, "I should have stayed away; then I wouldn't be here."

"You promised me I would be safe. That I had nothing to worry about," Casey blamed.

"You were never my child," said Mom.

"I can't believe I let my son near you," said Lyra.

I curled up as that and more swirled around me. Tears rolled down my face as I fought not to break down completely as my fears were being voiced out loud. My dad. My mom. Lyra. Ulric. Every person I cared about. Their voices swirled around me, laced with disgust as they said how much I disappointed them. That I was a mistake. That my very presence ruined their lives. How I should have been left on that church step. Or better yet, thrown into a dumpster. Woven through it all were the screams of my family and my friends. Each one was raw with pain and suffering, but all I could see was the vortex around me.

The crone sat at the edge of my vision. Through the swirling vortex, glimpses of her shone through. A distorted smile was plastered on the face as it grew younger. I shut my eyes and covered my ears, but the voices seemed to grow even louder.

"Rai!" yelled Tessa, but her voice was so far away and raspy, "Don't listen to them!"

My body responded to hers and uncurled itself. I couldn't get myself to block out the voices. I heard Tessa call my name over and over, but it was drowned out by the white noise in the background of everything else. My own voice started to mix in with the rest.

"I should just end it all now," came my voice.

"No!" I screamed at the vortex.

"Nobody cares about you," my voice seemed to answer me.

"Listen to yourself," said Ash. "It knows what's best."

"No, no, no," I cried.

Everything I had been holding back burst out as I began to sob uncontrollably. Ash didn't want me. Tessa hated me. Casey thought I was a freak. My parents would be better off had they had their own child and never found me. What was the point of staying where I was, with them? I could just transcend everything right now, like the sun wanted me to. They were dead already, and I hadn't been able to protect them. I felt the fire burning inside me, yet there was something different about it this time. It was a slow burn starting somewhere deep inside my soul and spread not just through my veins but something deeper.

"Rai! None of those voices are real!" yelled Ash. "Calm down!"

"We're still alive!" yelled Tessa.

"I love you!" yelled Ash and Tessa.

The fire inside me faded away, and the voices in the vortex seemed to get quieter.

"Ash? Tessa?" I called out hoarsely.

"We're here!" yelled Tessa.

"Silence," the crone said.

"We'll always be here!" yelled Ash.

"You too," said the crone.

I heard them both grunting to try and get my attention, but the crone's magic was keeping them silent. It was hard to block out the voices that still floated out from the swirling vortex, but I gritted my teeth and got to my knees.

"I refuse to be played like this," I grunted.

The magic seemed to intensify and speed up around me. The voices become a roaring cacophony and, for the most part, drown out any real words. It was almost deafening from the overstimulation of it all. But I knew the thoughts had been my own, and it kept me sitting there as my friends were tortured.

"Rai! I need you!" Casey yelled.

It was my fault they were in this mess. It was up to me to get them out. I pushed myself to my feet and watched as the smile on the now young woman's face turned into a frown. I stepped next to the vortex and took a deep breath. She looked confused as I stepped through it with ease.

Chapter Seventeen

"How? What are you?" asked the now young woman.

"You're not dealing with an average Scion warrior anymore," I mumbled gruffly.

I looked back at my family, who lay on the ground. Then to my friend who lay in their cage. The simple joke kept me from falling back into that pit of despair that was still so close to the surface. That feeling of failure that never truly went away. When I turned my attention back to the crone, she looked even more confused.

"It doesn't matter what I am. What matters is that if you don't stop siphoning the energy of my wife and husband, and stop killing my newest friend, I won't have a reason at all to hold back. I can unleash what I really want to," I growled.

"You can't hurt me," she laughed. "You're nothing to my power."

It's weird to feel your eyes burning with fire, yet still able to see perfectly.

"As the sun once told me. You. Are. Insignificant," I said through my teeth.

She fell back to the ground, and I stood over her.

"Let me go!" she pleaded.

"I just want to be left alone. I want my family to be left alone. I want my friends to be left alone. Is that clear?" I asked.

She nodded furiously.

"But above all that, there is something I want more. Do you know what that is?"

She looked up at me and slowly shook her head.

I walked over to Ash and bent down. He looked emaciated. His tan and muscles had all seemed to have been drained from him. His red hair was not as vibrant as normal. When I saw his chest move, it gave me a bit of relief. I touched him gently, and he stirred. Whatever that witch had been doing seemed to have stopped.

"Ash?" I asked tenderly.

"Rai?"

His voice was hoarse, and it looked like it took some effort to open his eyes, but he did.

"Let's get you up, love," I said.

It was slow, but I finally got him to stand on his own. I then went to Tessa. She looked like a corpse. Her once luscious hair was now just limp strands. Her pale skin was now gray and shriveled. I touched her, and her eyes shot open. Bloodshot and purple, she glared at me with a look of hunger.

"Take it easy, my darling," I murmured softly.

Slowly, she looked at me with recognition. I gave her a slight smile.

"Let's get you up, babe. You're looking good," I grinned.

I could tell she was ravenous, but she was keeping it under control the best she could. I took her to stand next to

Ash.

"Where is the key to the cage?" I asked the crone.

She pointed to a small desk with a shaky hand. I walked over to it and found a set of keys. It took a few tries until I finally found the right one. I don't know what I expected to see, but what I saw in that cage was not it. Casey seemed to have melted. When I touched them, they didn't move or register my touch. I scooped them out. It was hard to hold, and even harder to make sure their clothes stayed on. That they blinked at me was the only sign that told me they still lived. I handed them carefully to Ash.

"Get out of here now," I said and kissed him on the cheek.

He nodded at me even though I could tell he didn't want to listen to me. I turned to Tessa and kissed her forehead.

"I'll be out soon. Get to Isiak he will know what needs to be done for you," I said to her.

"I won't allow this," said the crone.

I spun to look at her. "I am talking to the people I love, so you will be quiet."

I turned around to Ash and Tessa and gave them a nod. They slowly made their way out as I walked back over to the crone.

"Now, where was I?" I asked.

"Letting me go," she said.

"Oh, right. That. So, you hurt Casey. Strike one. You hurt Tessa. Strike two. You hurt Ash. Strike three. You might be old but even you should know what happens after three strikes right?" I asked.

She started to crawl away from me. The house glowed as my body eclipsed the light from the fire.

"It means I am letting you go. Tell whatever god you pray to that this god said hello," I said.

I exploded in a flash of light. I hoped that everyone had gotten a safe distance. I don't know how long everything was black for me, but at some point, I was hovering over a pile of ash as Tessa and Ash knelt next to it. Ash looked a little better, still small but not as emaciated. Tessa looked completely normal. I guess whatever blood had been needed, she had gotten. I hope whoever she drank was okay. I crossed my ethereal arms and waited to be reborn. And I kept waiting. As they gathered the ash in a jar with a small broom and left, I was pulled along with it.

"Are they really dead this time?" Ash asked as he got into the limo beside Tessa.

"They can't be," said Tessa.

"It's been days," came Isiak's voice from the front. "I guess even gods have their limits."

"No! I'm right here!" I called out.

But of course, none of them heard me as I sat between them. Great, now I was a bloody ghost. First, a god who was useless, and now a ghost who was even more useless. Days passed, and I couldn't travel more than ten feet from my ashes, which sucked when they were locked in a basement. I waited for my funeral. Maybe they had one, and I hadn't seen it. You can't sleep as a ghost. It was no wonder that so many went insane. What were my parents going to think? If that funeral had happened and I came back, I would have to explain something I had never wanted to tell them. I paced around the room. It was all I could do. One day, Ash came down and stood by the jar.

"Come on, Rai. I don't want to believe you're dead for good, but it's been a week. I don't even know if you can hear me," said Ash.

"I can hear you. I think I might be dead. So much for the dream sun," I muttered.

"Tessa thinks you've moved on. Went to where the gods decide to hang out. But I don't buy that. Ain't no way you'd have left like that. You know those words you heard were lies, right?" asked Ash. "Your parents were always happy you were around. My parents even say that the Eckles were never happier than when they came back with their new child. Then me, you know how much I love you. Tessa feels the same. We'd be much different people without you."

I wanted to hug him. I didn't know a ghost could cry, but here I was doing so. I hovered next to him. I wanted to reach out and touch him, but I was also scared. What if I could touch him, but he didn't feel it? What if I just went through him? What if he felt my touch and then gave up on me? He left, and I stayed down there alone once again. A few minutes later, Isiak came down. I looked at him in confusion.

"Well, hello there," Isiak said as he turned to look at me.

"You can see me?" I exclaimed.

"Oh, most certainly I can," Isiak said with a shrug.

"How?"

"I am one of the oldest vampires that exist," Isiak said with a slight chuckle. "There are many things I can do that our young little Tessa has yet to be able to experience."

"So, am I dead?"

"I have no idea what you are. You're tied to your mortal remains, which is vastly different from a ghost."

"So, I am once again just an anomaly," I sighed.

"I do like having a little enigma around at my age."

"Well, I'm happy to be of use to someone," I said as I rolled my eyes.

Isiak laughed. I glared at him as he left. He had made me so annoyed that I forgot to ask about Casey. What had happened to them? What were they? I still had so many questions. I wasn't ready to be not dead but dead yet. I cursed the sun that had told me to ascend and leave everything behind. How could I even do that if I got stuck instead? Time passed, I couldn't say how long. Nobody came, and I felt like I was going to go insane. Then the twins came. John and Jane looked through me at the vase.

"What's that?" asked Jane.

"Has to be something awesome. Let's look," answered John.

Strange that they talk normally when they're alone. Then what they were going to do hit me.

"No. Don't play with my ashes," I said, and tried to grab them.

Of course, I went through. John picked up the vase as Jane took off the top.

"Eww, it's just a bunch of ash," said Jane.

John dropped the vase, spilling my ashes all over the

134

floor.

"Idiot!" said Jane.

"Who has ashes in a vase?" asked John. "That's weird."

"We have to put these back in before Ash sees it."

"Oh, right! He's been on edge lately."

They started to gather me up and put me back in. Much to my dismay, though, their hands were covered in me as they put the vase back up.

"Hurry, let's go wash up," Jane said as they ran off.

When they left, I paced around, wondering what would happen if part of my ashes were somewhere else. I tried to walk up the basement stairs, but didn't seem to be able to move any further. Go figure, it wouldn't matter. As I did something strange started to happen. To me, I was solid. Well, I looked solid anyway from my own perspective. But I started to get less so. As I paced, I looked at my feet, and suddenly I could see the floor through my foot.

"No, no, no," I muttered. "This can't be happening."

It started at my foot, but as the days passed, the rest of my body slowly followed until I was see-through. I grew more scared when my legs started to actually disappear. At one point, I floated around with just my eyes and up. I don't know what happened after my eyes disappeared. For what felt like an eternity, there was only darkness, even though I was conscious.

Then I woke up on the floor of the basement, completely naked. I sat up quickly and looked around. I ran my hands over my body to see if I was real. Not that it would have told me anything. I could feel my own skin, hair, and clothes when I was a not-ghost thing.

"What the hell?" I muttered.

My throat was dry, and I felt ravenous. I stood up on wobbly legs and went to the area I had been unable to cross. I hadn't felt anything like this, but I still expected to be pulled back as I put my leg forward. I yelled in triumph and relief as I stepped over that spot and closer to the stairs.

Before I could take another step, Tessa stood in front of me. Her face was filled with disbelief, and tears fell from her eyes. She reached out slowly, then pulled back. I could tell she didn't want to believe what her eyes saw. I stepped forward, and she flinched back.

"Tessa," I said, scratchily.

"This can't be you," she said quietly. "It's been too long."

"I'm me. How long has it been?" I asked as I continued forward.

"Two months," she said, and touched my chest.

My mouth fell open. No way had it been that long. How much of that time had I spent in darkness? She saw my reaction and came closer. Her arms wrapped around me almost too tightly. I hugged her back and kissed her forehead.

"I thought you were gone forever," she sobbed.

"You know me. Can't keep a good god down," I said.

She let go of me and slapped me gently. "Don't scare me like that again."

"Sorry," I muttered. "It wasn't my plan. At least you're safe."

"Barely," she said. "It was a few days before I could even come get your ashes."

Chapter Eighteen

I gently lifted her chin, and my lips met hers in a soft, tender kiss. She melted into me as our kiss deepened, and her tongue danced with mine. Her hands began a slow, tantalizing exploration of my body, setting my skin ablaze. With effortless strength, she pinned me against the wall. Her lips traced a cold path down my chest as her fingernail grazed my skin. It traced a line from my neck and down my torso as she teased my nipple with her mouth and sent a shiver through me. My fingers dug into her shirt as a moan escaped my lips as the pleasure rippled through me.

Her mouth continued, and each touch ignited a new flame within me. My hands fumbled with her clothes as I was desperate to feel her skin against mine. She chuckled low in her throat as she helped me discard her clothes in a hurried heap. Her body pressed against mine was cold but inviting. I groaned as my hips instinctively sought hers. She met me halfway, and our bodies moved in a rhythm as old as time itself. I broke away from her lips, gasping for air as I gazed into her eyes. They were filled with the same desire I felt.

"I've missed you," I whispered, my voice raw with emotion.

She smiled as her fingers traced my face. "I've missed you, too."

I captured her lips once more, pouring all my longing into the kiss. We stood there, bodies entwined, lost in the magic of our reunion. Our bodies moved in perfect harmony, a choreographed dance. I could feel the tension building, the pleasure coiling tighter and tighter. Suddenly, she gasped, her body shuddering against mine. I followed her over the edge as my release pulsed through me. I rested my forehead against hers, my ragged breathing the only sound around us. After a moment, she opened her eyes, and her gaze met mine.

"I love you," I whispered.

She smiled as her fingers gently combed through my hair. "I love you, too."

I pulled her close and held her. I didn't want to let her go ever again. Eventually, I had to, as my stomach made an audible growl.

She laughed and poked me, "Let's get you some clothes and food."

"Okay," I sighed.

Soon, I was dressed and eating everything I could get my hands on. There was leftover pizza, a peanut butter and jelly sandwich, some apples, and bananas, along with lots of water.

"Where's Ash?" I asked through bites of my sandwich.

"Took the twins out. It's the full moon," Tessa said as she watched me stuff my face with a little smile on her face from across the table.

I ate until I felt like I was going to burst and felt like trash. But I was finally feeling normal at the same time.

"So why are the twins here?" I asked. "They spilled my ashes all over the floor."

"What?" she exclaimed.

"Oh yea... I was like this ghost thing. Attached to my ashes. Until the twins came and dropped my ashes. When they put me back into the vase... I kinda started to vanish. I don't even know how long that lasted."

"I'm so sorry. I didn't know," Tessa said, and grabbed my hands from across the table.

"It's fine. I'm back now," I said. "But still, why are the twins here?"

"Oh. Yea. Ash decided that he wanted to bring them here to see if city life could calm them down some. We've also had a long talk with Isiak and the rest of the vampires. This will be a shared house. Vampires and Werewolves will be able to come and go as they please. But they need to stay in touch so that we know they've not fallen to the other side," said Tessa. "So there could or could not be an ever-changing group of people here at any time."

"Speaking of Isiak... where is he?"

Tessa shrugged and raised a brow. I wasn't sure I wanted to tell her that Isiak knew I was still around. At least not yet.

"I just want to ask him something. But it can wait," I said, and squeezed her hands.

We moved to the living room and put on Hamilton as we cuddled up. At some point, I realized I was now exhausted, and before I knew it, I was asleep. I woke up in my bed with Ash's arms wrapped around me. I moved to try and get up, and his arms tightened around me.

"Ash," I said softly. "I need to get up."

His arms slowly released me, and I kissed him gently

on the nose before slipping out of bed. A few minutes later, I returned. I sat on the edge and watched them—Ash curled loosely in the blankets, Tessa's hand resting near his shoulder, both of them lost in sleep. I would never give up on this. Nothing could ever make me want to. There had been a time I was afraid, terrified about how long I would live. I'd even questioned whether I should've left. Thinking it would be easier than watching them grow old and fade away as I went on, unchanging. But moments like this small, perfect scene made all those thoughts vanish. No matter the time we had left, these moments now were all that would matter to me, no matter how long I lived.

When my heart was full, I went downstairs to make breakfast. It felt like a different lifetime since I had last cooked, and I wanted that sense of normalcy. Besides, pancakes were quick and easy to make. I gathered what I needed. Flour, baking soda, sugar, milk, butter, eggs, and the saltshaker. I put them in a circle around a mixing bowl. My own little magic was about to happen. Three cups of flour, seven tablespoons of baking powder, and a teaspoon of salt went into the bowl. A stick of butter was melted in a microwave-safe bowl before I added it to the dry ingredients, followed by two and a half cups of milk, and two eggs.

Then I mixed it all together until it was smooth as I heated a lightly oiled griddle. When it was ready, I poured out the first spoonful—exactly a quarter cup for each. As I flipped the first pancake, the kitchen door burst open.

"What's that smell?" said John.

"Can we have some?" asked Jane.

"Sure," I said with a smile.

Ash came in after them and I could tell by his look the smell had woken him and brought him also. I looked at the batter and realized I hadn't made enough for ravenous growing wolves and laughed. At least I hadn't put everything away. Once I was done with the few I had on the griddle, I doubled the ingredients in a second mixing bowl and made more before I continued. Before long, the young wolves were out with heaping stacks to do whatever they did, and I sat across from Ash with our own plates.

"I never gave up," Ash said quietly.

"I know," I murmured. "I was still here… just not able to be seen."

Ash frowned. "So, you were dead?"

"I don't think so. I don't really know."

"Did you see anything?"

"Not particularly. It was all darkness. Then I was back at that house. Then I went with y'all when you took the ashes to the basement."

"Oh," Ash said, slightly disappointed.

"Like I said, I wasn't truly dead. So, there could be something."

"I'm just glad you're back. Now you can help me with those two."

"No, no, no. I'm not getting on their bad side. I like my eyebrows."

"They only did that once. To a slumber party," laughed Ash.

"They're demons," I laughed. "So, how did you get

them here?"

"Their parents transferred them to school here. I didn't want to be away from you anymore, just because of them. But I'm also now their legal guardian. So, guess you're now a parent," Ash laughed.

I groaned, and he laughed louder. John and Jane ran back into the dining room in a panic, saw us, and just started walking as they went out the other door.

"Well, I better go see what that's about," Ash said as he got up.

I smiled at him, and he smiled back before he followed them. A few seconds later, a werewolf named Sam ran in. I almost didn't recognize who it was as he was completely hairless. He had once had a large bushy beard, unkempt eyebrows, and hair that I swore birds had nested in. I just shrugged as he looked around at the doorways that left the area. I laughed quietly as he took the wrong door. I guess what had removed his hair had also made his sense of smell haywire. As I sat there, I thought of Casey. I had no phone to talk to them, and I didn't even know if they were still alive. I also needed to speak to Isiak, but that would need to wait until night. So, I set about cleaning up the plate left by Ash and the mess I had made in the kitchen.

The day moved by slower than I thought possible as I cleaned. Summer was over, and Casey would be back in class. The problem was that I didn't know their schedule. But I was willing to bet that after everything, night classes would be the last thing on their mind. So, I had at least another day to get my mind together to talk to Isiak before going to them. Of course, the slow day probably happened to be mostly because we had a whole staff that cleaned everything, so I mostly just got in their way and was shooed away.

Throughout the house were also Ash's family members, who were on a never-ending search for the twins. I made a point to buy new shampoo and…well, everything I owned. Some were itching from itching powder put in their clothes, some had their hair cut badly, and some, like Sam, had their hair removed with something. It did make me laugh every time I saw one, though. I eventually found Ash and the twins. Ash had cornered them up a tree.

"I told you two to stop it with the tricks," Ash scolded.

"Sure, but it's not tricks, it's pranks," the twins said in unison.

"You know what I meant!" Ash said through gritted teeth.

"How are we supposed to know what you mean if you don't say what you mean?" they said and shrugged.

"I'm not going to stop them if they find you."

"We can take care of the family."

"Though when the vampires wake up…" said Jane.

"We're going to be out running at night, right?" asked John.

"What did you do to the vampires?" asked Ash, worried.

"Nothing," the twins said sweetly, with big smiles.

"Oh God, why me?" Ash asked as he banged his head against the tree.

"How's it going, pops?" I asked with a laugh.

"Don't you start."

I gave him a quick kiss and scampered away while he went back to scolding the twins, who paid him no attention. As night came, the werewolves were gone, and I was in the middle of watching a movie when a lot of screeches were heard. Suddenly, Tessa, Isiak, Corri, and half a dozen other vampires were around me.

"Where are those dogs?" asked Keiyana, a vampire I hadn't met before.

Tattooed on her face were the words 'Dogz Rool Batz Drule.'

"That's a nice look," laughed Isiak.

As I looked at the other vampires, they also had things tattooed on their faces. I didn't even know how that was possible with the whole touching a vampire while they slept was meant to get you attacked.

"We're going to kill those dogs," said Hannah.

"Take it easy. I'm sure we can work something out," said Tessa.

"Why are you four perfectly okay?" asked Shawn.

"We board our room up," said Corri. "We have heard those twins are terrorists."

"The twins are probably working up to me and Tessa," I said. "They just need to see how far they can get before it gets too far."

"Well, keep them out of our rooms. If we see them, we will take our ire out on them," said Hannah.

"Noted," said Tessa. "I'll make sure it gets dealt with."

And just as quickly as I was surrounded, it was just me,

Isiak, Corri, and Tessa.

"So, I see you're doing well. Corporal and everything now," said Isiak.

'What do you mean?" asked Tessa.

"He could see me," I said dryly.

Her eyes glowed purple as she turned to him.

"I did say he was fine," Isiak replied with a slight shrug.

Tessa turned and stormed out.

"One day, you're going to push her too far. You're about as bad as the twins," I said.

"Oh, you worry about me?" said Isiak sarcastically.

"Nope. Just waiting until you're finally gone. So, will you tell me now what Casey is?"

"Oh, that. Did you not figure it out those months you were unable to do anything but think? From what I hear, you saw a fairy in one of those cages of that mage. They are part of the fae world. It is a very rare thing to be seen in our world."

"Are you telling me they're fae?" I asked, slack-jawed.

"Mostly. They're a changeling," said Corri.

"What? As in the thing from that tabletop RPG? Can they change into anything they want?"

"What? Not anything," scoffed Isiak. "They're fae-born left behind as infants. When babies are stolen, sometimes, it's by the fae. Most of the time, they leave behind glamoured pieces of wood, unless they have an aging fae they wish to be rid of. But on very rare occasions, they leave behind babies of their own, which have become known as Changelings. They are meant to be reclaimed later, though I suppose they don't always return, if your friend is any proof."

"How do you tell someone that…?" I asked quietly.

"That is not a thing I ever have to worry about," smiled Isiak.

"Do they have any enemies? Like how werewolves and vampires are? Cause they were stalked by something that had wings and red eyes," I said.

"That I don't know. Vampires wouldn't go after those creatures. They have a very acidic smell. It would be like… eating what you call battery acid," said Isiak. "Though anything is possible. I don't make it a priority to know what stalks what; just what things are. More so after meeting you, and Yujin's death."

Chapter Nineteen

The next night, I stood in front of Casey's door. I must have stood there for ten minutes as I tried to get the courage to knock on the door. What did they think? Did they know I had been dead for months? Did they think I abandoned them? I stood there with my hand hovering above the door when it opened. A girl with dark skin, purple-black lipstick, bloodshot eyes, and red hair stood in front of me.

"Oh, who are you?" she asked with a slight smirk.

"Uhm... Rai," I stumbled over my words.

"Ah, so you do exist," she said. "Well, I'm off. Casey, it's for you."

She walked by me without another look, and I watched her go with a look of confusion. I stumbled forward as I was tackled with a hug from behind.

"I thought you were dead!" she exclaimed.

"I was," I chuckled a little sadly.

She let me go, and I turned around. I smiled brightly. She looked much better than last time I saw her. I gave her a big hug.

"You look great, compared to... You know. What happened to you?" I asked.

"I... don't know. It was like I couldn't keep my form together. It was strange."

"You're looking fine, though," I said with a small hit

148

with my shoulder against her.

She laughed and looked down, "You're looking better than I saw you last time, too."

"Hey, I think I look best when I'm dust," I said with a shrug.

She looked up at me with a disappointed look on her face.

"Sorry."

"It's okay," she said and pulled me inside the room.

"So… I've found out what you are," I said once we were inside.

"You did? I thought I was a demigod?"

"Seems like… I have a lot to learn."

"Well, what am I?"

"A fae. A Changeling is what you were called."

"Are you sure?" she asked.

"Like I said, it's what I was told. I just thought with the abilities you'd be like me. A god. But it seems like you're a fairy creature."

She sat on her bed, looking sad.

"So… there was a little baby that I replaced? What would have happened to it?"

"You know what those are?"

"Yes," she said quietly.

"I don't really know the specifics of anything," I admitted as I sat next to her.

"Nothing good ever happens to the ones in the stories.

And… what if that's why my… or this person I stole the life of… dad was taken by the fae also? If they came in when I was being put in their place, they could have easily turned him into something and taken him also. What if the person my mother loved didn't abandon her?"

"It's not any use thinking about what could have been," I said as I wrapped an arm around her shoulders.

She leaned against me. "So, want to tell me how you're married to a werewolf and a vampire? That seems like a story."

I told her about the strange ritual that Yujin had put on.

"Technically, in the eyes of those clans, we are… but I'm not sure if the ritual counted me. It's too complicated for even me. They shared minds. Since magic doesn't work for me, I don't know what they did exactly," I explained.

"If magic doesn't work on you… What happened in the house?" she asked.

"Your guess is as good as mine. I'm guessing that since I can see it happen, I can hear it happen, and it was all just auditory using just the normal insecurities people have," I shrugged.

"For what it's worth… I don't think you failed me."

"Thanks," I said with a slight smile. "I'm glad you don't think I left you. I don't have many friends and don't want to lose any."

"I was angry for a while. Then the torture and thinking you were dead… eased that."

"Well, thank you for forgiving me. I know I put you through a lot. But… I do wish I knew what came after you.

Wasn't a vampire or a werewolf, I do know that."

"I haven't seen it again. Though I try to stay inside at night these days."

"I don't blame you. Staying inside at night does make it harder for things to come after you. Though… your roommate… where is she going all alone?"

"Probably where she always goes," Casey shrugged.

"Well, how about we get lunch the next day you're free?" I asked.

"Tomorrow?" she asked.

"Deal. I'd stay longer, but… being dead for months kinda… need to spend time with the family."

"I'd say be safe out there, but it seems you'll always be fine."

"That's me. Forever fine," I smiled and stood up.

After a quick hug, I was on my way home. When I walked through the door to the mansion, the twins were tied up in the foyer.

"What happened here?" I asked with a raised brow.

"We got caught," they said in unison. "Want to let us go?"

"Well, have fun," I said and stepped over them.

"Ooo, Rai, wait until we get free!" they called out.

"Maybe you should have looked at the walls before you decided to put Saran Wrap in the hallway," I called out as I continued down the hall.

"You!" they yelled.

I laughed as they cursed at me. I ran into Ash as he rounded a corner in a panic.

"Rai? Have you seen the twins? I let them out of my sight for two minutes, and nobody has seen them," said Ash.

"Check the foyer," I said, and kissed him. "Then, when you do, come find me."

"Well… they can wait," he said and pushed me against the wall.

My fingers ran through his hair as he kissed me hard. His lips were warm and demanding as they pressed against mine with a passion that left me breathless. I could feel his heart beating in his chest as it mirrored the frantic beat of my own. His hand roamed my body, telling me that he wanted more. Every touch as we kissed made my body hotter, and I moaned as we kissed. I arched against his body, and he pulled me closer. The pure and simple raw desire.

"Must you people do that in the open?" scoffed Isiak.

Ash backed away, and I pouted. I looked at Isiak and sighed.

"You're right," I said and grabbed Ash by the hand.

I eagerly tugged on his hand and led him towards our room, with hope that I would see Tessa there too. As we stepped over the threshold of the room, Ash effortlessly swept me into his strong arms and carried me to bed. I clung to him, my arms wrapped around his neck, as he gently laid me down onto the soft sheets. Without hesitation, I leaned up to capture his lips in a passionate kiss.

"I love you," I murmured.

A smile slowly spread over his lips, and he said, "I

know."

His skilled hands roamed my body, which stoked the desire inside of me even higher. The air around us seemed to crackle with desire. Each touch and soft kiss fueled the passion that built between us. Tessa entered the room quietly, her presence adding to the already intense atmosphere. Her eyes glinted with lust as she took in the scene before her, and she slowly made her way towards us. As my clothes were ripped off, she lowered herself onto the bed beside us with a devious smirk. As her finger ran up my outstretched arm, my body responded eagerly to her touch. Ash kissed down my body, and I let out soft moans as I watched Tessa slowly undress herself. My back arched as Ash reached between my legs, and Tessa's fingers tangled themselves in my hair. Her lips connected with mine, stifling a loud moan. Ash's large hands ran up my body as his tongue flicked teasingly around me. My hips moved toward him, wanting more.

As Tessa pulled away from me, my fingers were left grasping at thin air. She smirked and moved out of reach as she teased me with her alluring presence. I moaned as Ash continued his tantalizing dance with his tongue and mouth. She positioned herself above my head, and her hips swayed sensually as I wrapped my hands around her legs. She slowly sat down onto my face and slowly ground against my mouth. The sweet, intoxicating scent of her filled my senses, urging me to taste her. I eagerly licked and sucked on her as soft moans of my name escaped her lips. The hours went by slowly as we stayed in that bed, pleasuring each other, wanting to be in and near each other.

Chapter Twenty

Everything was chaos as the months drifted by. The younger vampires who had come in had declared war on the twins. It got so bad with the pranks, tricks, and everything else that we had to section off a part of the house for them to continue their war in. It kept the twins occupied and somehow less rowdy, while making sure there were areas that were off-limits. A place where the older of us could be left alone. Most of us had grown tired of needing to watch our every step so that we didn't get hurt. I had personally been glued to a wall for most of a day because Ash had been at his classes, and Tessa had been asleep. I think one werewolf was still missing half a toe.

Every day, Ash would say he didn't know if the werewolves would stay. That the animosity was getting high. Yet as time went by, more and more showed up. The younger werewolves had even become friendly with the young-looking vampires, some of whom were probably still actually young and newly turned. However, that alliance had been formed in part as a coalition against the twins. A common enemy always forged the most unlikely of bonds. The house was almost full of wolves, vampires, and humans when my favorite holiday came around.

Now you might think to yourself, "Hey, Halloween, that's your favorite holiday". Well, you would have been right a few years ago. Over the last year, though, one day had risen to the top. Thanksgiving. Now hear me out, sure, Halloween has the better movies, and the better atmosphere, but I basically lived in one of those movies. Werewolves to the left, vampires to the right, and I'm just stuck in the middle. Don't get me wrong, I loved sitting on the couch, nestled between Ash and Tessa as we watched whatever new horror movie was on one of the million streaming services. And when Ash would answer the door to give out candy in his wolfman form, the oohs and aahs from the children brought smiles to the three of our faces. Even the parents would be impressed and ask where he had gotten his costume. He would, of course, just tell them it was custom-made and leave it at that.

Thanksgiving, though, was a time to be grateful for the ones you loved, what you had, and for your family. And my family was enormous now. Not like when I grew up, when my parents and I would not do much for it. My parents thought it was a terrible day that represented all that was wrong in the world. I was determined not to let it be about the things of the past and just make it about the people who meant everything to me. Though my parents wouldn't come, they were always around in my heart anyway. On top of all that, I got to do the one thing I loved doing, cooking. Sure, there's Christmas, but it didn't have that same feeling to it. There were so many Christmas movies and songs everywhere, it was easy to see the commercialization of it, no matter where you turned. Thanksgiving had an easier time tuning that side of it out.

The twins and the wolf/vampire coalition had declared a ceasefire for that whole week leading up to Thanksgiving. Mostly because I had threatened to let Ash do the cooking if they didn't. And as the twins had so eloquently put it, nobody wanted to eat burnt yet still raw steaks for Thanksgiving. The day was meant to have as many options available as there were stars in the sky. The day of, I worked from sunup to sundown, making sure everything was perfect. I can't take all the credit, though; I had help from some of the other staff who could cook. Still, I felt like a head chef as I tasted everything, pointed out what was missing when needed, and generally ensured it met my standards for the late-night meal.

There was ham, turkey, fried and roasted chicken, duck, bison, an array of different beef, deer, as well as apple pie, pecan pie, cherry pie, pumpkin pie, and cake. A dozen different types of cookies and cakes were also available, along with numerous side dishes. We had candied yams, sweet potatoes, potato salad, crab cakes, egg salad, deviled eggs, mashed potatoes, baked potatoes, curly fries, steak fries, crinkle cut fries, green bean casserole, stuffing, corn, okra, cabbage, salad, fruit salad, and a whole other assortment of vegetable platters. It was nice when you had a kitchen the size of a large apartment, complete with all the equipment a Michelin-starred restaurant would have.

The anticipation had been building all day, and finally, the time came for the long-awaited feast. With everyone's help, it was all set out and ready for the merged family to gather. The wolves, the maids, and the butlers had all filled the room I had dubbed the Feasting Hall. I knew I was starving, and I was sure the rest felt the same. From the vampire's side, it was just Tessa and a handful of others, those who had truly become friends with the werewolves thanks to the alliance they had formed against the twins.

"I'm so glad I can be here with most of my newfound family. It doesn't matter if you're a werewolf or a vampire, I'm glad you're all here and that some of you have put aside the prejudices of the older generation to see that we can all get along," I said as I carved the turkey.

"I'm just thankful that this holiday season is here. I'm losing track of all the creatures that are starting to show up at school," said Ash. "And I already had enough trouble telling what was what."

"What?" I blinked. "Why are more of the supernatural invading our town?"

Ash looked at me and slowly blinked back.

"What?" I repeated.

"Did you think that a whole surf team of werewolves, you, and Casey were all random coincidences?"

"I did... until two seconds ago."

"Dear, it's a college for our kind," laughed Ash. "A place where the supernatural can go, get an education, and not be found out. All the cliques in there? Just different types of creatures sticking together."

"Oh," I said and sagged my shoulders.

"Even we knew that," said the twins.

"Don't you brats start," I muttered.

"Mom, Rai's being mean to us," whined the twins.

"I'm not your Mom," groaned Tessa.

"Dad, Mom's being mean to us."

"I'm not your Dad," Ash said, exasperated.

"Rai, Mom and Dad are being mean to us."

"Well, how rude of them," I said in mock indignation. "Guess I'll just have to spank them for that."

'Rai!" Ash and Tessa shouted together.

Amidst a chorus of groans from everyone else, I

flashed a sweet smile at my spouses and returned to finish carving the mouth-watering turkey so that everyone could start getting their food. The aroma of the food filled the air along with the chatter and laughter of friends and family. The night was alive with merriment and joy. For me, it was cut short as by the time I finished my plate, I was about to crash and had trouble keeping my eyes open. Midnight had crept up on us, the hours having flown by. The full day of cooking had left me exhausted, and I was the first to leave. I had just drifted off into a dream where I walked along the surface of the sun when Tessa gently shook me awake, bringing me back to reality.

"Is it morning already?" I muttered and rubbed my eyes.

"Not quite. Someone's at the door for you," replied Tessa, a bit of worry in her voice.

"Can it wait until morning?" I grumbled and closed my eyes.

"They seem pretty insistent on seeing you."

I yawned and got out of bed. I shuffled to get dressed and then to the front door. When I got there, Ash waited with a confused look on his face.

"What's going on?" I mumbled.

"I wish I knew," answered Ash, "They refused to leave until you came."

"Are they anything I should be worried about?" I asked, followed by a yawn.

"They're… human? Maybe… I don't know," Ash said uncertainly.

"I think so," added Tessa. "But they're also… different."

"Well, guess it's time to say hello," I sighed and put my hand on the door handle.

I took a deep breath and quickly pulled open the door. In front of me was the oldest man I had ever seen. His ancient features were etched with deep lines and wrinkles. His skin was rich and dark, almost blending into the shadows around him. He was hunched over, tiny, and frail-looking. His hair was wispy white, and liver spots covered his skin. In contrast to him was a woman of middle age with a rosy complexion and long, flowing auburn hair that fell to the ground. They stood arm in arm, but she wasn't exactly helping him stand; it was just how they stood. Despite his aged appearance, the man seemed to be full of youth. He smiled at me with a toothless grin that seemed to radiate. Her smile was more reserved, but still seemed to shine just as bright.

"Uhm… hi?" I managed, my eyes flicking between them.

"It's so nice to finally see you," said the man warmly.

My mind reeled. That voice… There was no way it was the same as my dream.

"Who are you?" I asked.

"I think you know the answer to that," the woman replied.

Her voice, while soft, also seemed to echo inside my head.

"Oh, I'm sure it'll come to them any minute now. This

one's a sharp one," chuckled the man.

"I've heard your voice before," I whispered. "But there's no way it could have been."

"All my avatars carry my voice," he explained with a wink.

"But you were a sun," I said hesitantly.

"I am one of many stars in the sky above. And many other things," the old man replied cryptically.

"He does like to ride around in my chariot," the woman smiled.

"Oh, that was how we met. And now they accuse you of dragging my avatars around," the man laughed.

"Okay, stop. No. Tell me what's going on here," I demanded.

"Why, we came for Thanksgiving, of course. Thought we'd be part of this family you've put together," said the woman matter-of-factly.

"Well, it's kinda late. And dinner is kinda over," I said flatly. "Guess there is next year."

"I told you we should have come sooner," she muttered.

"I was busy. These things are hard to do when you're trapped somewhere asleep," said the man with a shake of his head.

"Who are you?!" I asked in frustration.

They were making no sense to me, and I was sleepy. The last thing I wanted to do was stand in a doorway while two old people argued with each other.

"Maybe they're not as sharp as I thought. To think they almost ascended to our realm, too," the man mused.

"We did wake them up," said the woman. "I know how cranky I can be until the sun is up."

"Yes. You did wake me up. Now you say you want to be part of a family and get together, but I don't know you. We're not related. There's nothing that can be done for you."

"But we are family. The only family that will be with you when the pup and the bat fade from memory," the man stated. "I thought you would have gotten it when I came to you as the sun itself, but I overestimated how much you know."

"You're Ra," Tessa said in a low voice from behind me. 'So that must mean you're... Eos."

"Aurora. Eos and I are not the same," corrected the woman with a heavy sigh.

I turned my head to look at Tessa. She gave me a slight nod to tell me whatever I was thinking was right. Ash stood next to her with a look of confusion written all over his face. Like he had expected the conversation to go a different way. My own mind was not comprehending anything that was being said. Slowly, as if my brain had finally woken up, my thoughts finally caught up with the gravity of the situation. I turned back to the two people at the doorway and stared at them with awe.

"My parents!" I exclaimed.

"Now they get it," Ra chuckled.

"I like her. She's smart. Do try to keep her around," Aurora smirked.

"Why did you come now? After so long?" I snapped.

As soon as the realization of who they were hit me, a wave of boiling anger surged through me like a raging inferno. The betrayal and the abandonment I had felt overtook me. My heart pounded in my chest, and I clenched my fists at my sides. I struggled to contain the raw emotion that threatened to spill out, but eventually it was too much.

"You can't just come here after all this time and act like everything is fine! You're not allowed to just show up when and how you want and expect me to care—or even want to meet you!"

"Now, Phoenix, we can't just rush off and meet all of our children," said Ra gently. "It's hard enough for me to be conscious long enough to do even this."

"Why do you seem human?" Ash asked from over my shoulder.

"So that your kind leaves us alone. We seem human enough, but also odd enough that you don't look too closely at us," explained Aurora. "As for you, my child, we are not the type of beings that raise anything. You were never meant to be in this realm or look like that. But what happened cannot be changed. I'm only here because Ra insisted."

"Thanks for the effort," I said dryly.

"You almost broke the barrier of what you are, to become what you should be. That brought my attention to you," continued Aurora.

"You have a way of… invading my dreams," added Ra. "I've seen some of your life. You've dreamt of the sun, and even that dream version is part of me. Sometimes. So, I thought I would give you help when you needed it most."

"I don't need your help, and I don't want to ascend or anything like that," I growled and moved to shut the door.

Ash caught it and looked at me.

"Come in. Maybe we can have a little bit of leftovers," Ash offered.

"Whatever," I muttered, turning away.

Ra and Aurora walked in and followed me to the dining room. Ash and Tessa made us sit at a small table and wouldn't let me get up to get any food. They warmed it up, brought it out, and placed it in front of us.

"Rai cooked this. They're great at it," Ash noted as he served us.

"The Phoenix is always good with fire," remarked Aurora.

"Are there others?" Tessa asked.

"Phoenix? Of course. How else do you think those legends happened? Are they my children? No. I didn't even know what you would be," answered Aurora.

"They are our only child," clarified Ra.

"Great, so I don't have any siblings," I grumbled.

"You have plenty of half-siblings," Ra responded.

"The Rain, the Air, and the Four Winds," added Aurora.

"Oh, great, I'll just go talk to the fresh air right now. Then I'll see what they think of you two," I said with a scowl.

"She means Shu, Tefnut, and the Venti—Aquilo, Favonius, Auster, and Vulturnus. Though you have others too. Mafdet, Anhur, Maat, Bastet, and Sekhmet. But, they don't fit that same theme," explained Tessa.

"Doesn't matter to me. You two can show yourselves out."

I stormed out and down the hall. Ash followed me.

"Babe…" he put a hand on my shoulder. "This could be your only chance to finally talk to them."

"We talked. I wanted to know why they left, and I found out. They basically told me GG's," I said in frustration.

He gently turned my body towards him, and his strong arms enveloped me. He had grown back nearly all the muscle mass he had lost from the crone. I buried my face in his chest. My quiet sobs wracked my body as I cried against him. He lovingly rubbed soothing circles on my back as I did. I didn't stop crying silently until I heard a door shut, and Tessa gently touched my arm. When that happened, my suppressed wails erupted from me as I broke down even more. I realized I had ruined any chance to get to know them. My anger towards Ra and Aurora had been too much, and now it had been replaced with pure devastation in my soul. I had tried to be silent because I hadn't wanted to give Ra or Aurora the knowledge that they had affected me so completely. I knew it was selfish and foolish, but in that moment, logic fell to the wayside as raw emotions overpowered me when I realized who they truly were. I wanted to talk to them and get to know them. I had also yearned for them to want me. To be the family that I had longed for my whole life. Not to just appear and tell me that they hadn't cared until I had almost left my family. I tired myself out quickly from the crying and fell asleep in Ash's comforting embrace.

Epilogue

As Rai and Tessa slept, I watched over them from a large chair in the corner of the room. Rai had cried themselves to sleep, and Tessa had fallen into her daytime slumber. I completely understood why Rai had done what they did, but I wished they had talked to their parents more. We already knew that gods were terrible as parents. I guessed Rai hadn't fully accepted that, even after being told that gods were infamous for abandoning their kids without a second thought. It was a dysfunctional family, one where their children ended up trying to kill them. Rai was much better off without being around that.

When Tessa went to wake Rai, I was able to talk with Ra and Aurora. I hadn't known who they were, but their message was clear enough. Even for me. They had come to warn Rai—something big was coming. For the last year and a half, we had only been worried about threats simply because they had come to mess with our lives. Maybe Yujin had known something bigger was on the horizon. Maybe that was why he had tried to unite my pack with his clan. That's something none of us will ever know, I guess.

All I know is that after warning me, two gods had praised Yujin's decision to combine a clan of vampires with a pack of werewolves. They also thanked me for having stayed by Rai's side all these years. They told me Rai would need the full might of our family in the near future.

As I sat there and watched Tessa and Rai sleep, I made a silent vow—I would sacrifice everything to make sure they were never hurt again. I was not going to lose Rai again. Those two months without them had been rough… agonizing. I hadn't just lost a partner; I had lost my best friend. It had been said countlessly that they were immortal, but I wasn't sure I believed that anymore. We still didn't know how they had come back alive. What if it's two years next time? What if they didn't come back at all? I couldn't risk that.

And Tessa… she would outlive me, but she wasn't immortal. She'd risk her own life for Rai or me, without hesitation, same as I would for either of them. I had to make sure that didn't happen. I intended to make sure I was the first to go, from old age and not in battle. No matter the cost, I was going to keep both of them safe.

The End

LEGACY OF LONELINESS

Also By Olyn Moon

In This Series

Blood and Moonlight: Legacy of Embers
(Book 1)

Other Books

Kill Kasan

Shadows and Vengeance: The Saga of Rekka Hoshi

About The Author

Olyn Moon is a Texan writer with a flair for storytelling, heavily influenced by the vibrant world of Japanese animation. Just like anime, Olyn loves to mix it up, dabbling in various genres from fantasy to sci-fi and everything in between. When not lost in the realms of writing, you'll likely find Olyn lost in the world of Tabletop RPGs or deep in the fantasy worlds of video games.

www.ingramcontent.com/pod-product-compliance
Lightning Source LLC
Chambersburg PA
CBHW060116260626
47160CB00005B/1902